"GO TO HELL, DEVLIN DOUGLAS! THAT'S WHERE YOU BELONG!"

"If I do go, Erin—" His words were hot, white-hot, and each letter of each word burned the imprint of its fevered promise into her body. She could feel the singeing heat of his passion as it flowed over her like fire and brimstone, punishing at the same time that it was caressing her sensuously. "You'll go with me. You can't escape. I won't let you."

His eyes dared her to defy him. His hand clasped her shoulder, the touch searing through the silk to her flesh. She knew that with the touch he had claimed her soul and marked her with his burning fire. She knew that she was a marked woman. And if Devlin Douglas were the devil, she belonged to him.

A CANDLELIGHT ECSTASY ROMANCE ®

LOVING BRAND

Emma Bennett

A CANDLELIGHT ECSTASY ROMANCE ®

To Our Readers:

We have been delighted with your enthusiastic response to Candlelight Ecstasy Romances®, and we thank you for the interest you have shown in this exciting series.

In the upcoming months we will continue to present the distinctive sensuous love stories you have come to expect only from Ecstasy. We look forward to bringing you many more books from your favorite authors and also the very finest work from new authors of contemporary romantic fiction.

As always, we are striving to present the unique, absorbing love stories that you enjoy most—books that are more than ordinary romance.

Your suggestions and comments are always welcome. Please write to us at the address below.

Sincerely,

The Editors
Candlelight Romances
1 Dag Hammarskjold Plaza
New York, New York 10017

CHAPTER ONE

As Erin walked into the lounge of the quaint restaurant on the outskirts of Houston, she saw Raymond seated at the bar. Smiling at the familiar figure, she lifted her hand, caressing the black and gold choker around her neck. As she moved across the room, she shifted her leather portfolio, tucking it under her elbow, and she brushed her fingers against the smooth blond hair that was beautifully swept upward from her neck and face in a chignon of curls.

Raymond turned his head just as Erin appeared, a friendly grin creasing the sun-browned face. "I do believe, Erin Lindsay," he teased in a deeply mellow voice that was slightly tinged with laughter, "you grow more beautiful every time I see you. Shame I'm not your type!"

Erin chuckled softly with him, shaking her head. "If ever I thought you were serious, Raymond DeLaGarza," she warned him, "I might take you up on that. But you're too big a flirt for me to believe you."

"Big for sure," he laughed, patting his tummy. Then he swept his hand up, motioning her to join him. "Care for a drink?"

"White wine," Erin replied with a slight nod, following his gaze, searching for a secluded booth so they could talk.

After they had ordered their drinks and had seated themselves away from the hubbub of the milling crowd, Raymond spoke, a reflective thoughtfulness in his voice. "I suppose you're wondering why the urgency of this meeting today."

"Umm-hmm," Erin soughed, sipping her wine. When no quick answer was forthcoming, she lifted her face. "More especially," she augmented, tapping her hand on her portfolio, "I'm wondering why you asked me to review my files on the Cortez-Hernandez contract, and I'm wondering why you suggested that I bring my copies of the paperwork with me."

Raymond laughed, inclining his head, his hair gleaming a blue-black in the November sunlight that streamed through the window. "Never one to equivocate, are you, Erin?"

Her eyes, light blue in the center, were rimmed in deep midnight, and they twinkled with life. "We've been doing business together too long for us to play games, old friend."

Raymond lifted a stubby hand, rubbing his index finger over the thick moustache that shadowed his upper lip. "That's what makes you stand so tall in the business world," he admired her openly. "You always go to the heart of the matter." He sighed theatrically, lifting his large shoulder. "And I so thought I could finally impress you with the beautiful atmosphere of Quail Ridge Dairy Farm before we began to talk business."

"You have," Erin quipped cheerfully. "It's indeed beautiful." She set her glass down, allowing her eyes to travel around the dairy-turned-restaurant. "Cozy and unique." She pushed up the sleeves of her elegant red silk jacket. "The calico curtains are authentically old-fashioned, the dairymaids who are scurrying about are lovely, and the dairy implements hanging on the wall are interesting as well as ornamental, but—" She droned the last word softly, not quite turning it loose, and she lifted a finely arched brow. "There's just so much that one can say about it, and—" her voice was full of expressive indulgence "—I've covered it all."

Raymond nodded, lowering his head, fiddling with his drink. Finally he looked up, levelly meeting Erin's steadfast gaze. Still he didn't speak.

"Something's wrong with the bidding, isn't it?"

Raymond shifted his weight on the chair, and his brow furrowed with thought as his gaze once again swept around the room before it came to rest on Erin's cool countenance. Shrewdly he studied the woman who sat across from him, eventually saying, "You know that as of last year when Cortez bought controlling interest and became the senior partner with Hernandez, their firm became the largest in South America." He paused. "And it's one of the most influential in all Latin America. A contract with them can make or break you. And it's worth whatever you have to do to get it."

"So far, Raymond," Erin softly reminded him, "you've just repeated what I already know. Surprise me. Tell me something new."

"Getting edgy?" he teased.

"No, but I think you are," she returned gently, gracefully cradling her glass in both hands.

Her blue eyes steadily stared into his brown ones, and she quirked her lips into that smile that Raymond so easily recognized and succumbed to. She was tense; there was no denying that. But she had learned during the thirteen years that she had worked with Lindsay Machinery to discipline her emotions. And in the year since she'd become president, she had governed her anxieties and apprehensions well, channeling her stress into productive energy, letting her business acumen speak for itself. Because of her control she had no fear when her eyes caught and held those of Raymond DeLaGarza. He could read no more than what she deliberately wrote there for him to see.

"Are you nervous, Raymond?"

He nodded. "I am."

"Why?"

"Your bid was well received, and it was one of the better ones. One of the final two, I may add."

Erin chuckled softly, forcing herself to sound happier than she felt. "But it wasn't the best," she filled in, "and you invited me to lunch to break the bad news gently."

"Not really," he contradicted her slowly. "I invited you to lunch to discuss the contract because I was invited to lunch to discuss it."

"Come again," she quipped. "I'm not following you too well."

"We were invited to lunch to defend and to explain our bid."

Erin's face mirrored her surprise. "Hernandez?"

"No! Cortez. He's reviewing the bids, not Hernandez."

"And?"

"He's invited you and Devlin to lunch so that—" he paused, searching for the right words "—so that you can give a verbal explanation of your offers."

"And you agreed!" Erin expostulated vehemently.

"I agreed," he affirmed quietly, not the least put out by her indignation.

Erin was furious. In the three years since she had employed the Raymond DeLaGarza Agency to submit her Latin American bids, he had never pulled anything like this. "You should have asked me first," she protested. "I think this is totally unorthodox. I've never been involved in—in—open bidding before."

"There's always a first time for everything," Raymond explained. "And this was the right time for the first time."

He grinned at his witticism. "Cortez-Hernandez received two outstanding bids. The one I submitted for you, and one that Devlin Douglas submitted."

"And they liked his better?" Erin questioned.

"Cortez did, but Hernandez favored yours."

"Surely they'll take my successful record into consideration," she mused.

"They have. But rumor has them running scared."

"Rumor shouldn't affect their decision that much," Erin scoffed. "My work has been satisfactory in the past. My products are delivered on time, and they are always of the finest quality. I don't think any of my customers have had reason to complain about either service or quality."

"That's not the kind of rumor that we're talking about," Raymond quietly pointed out. "There are rumors circulating about a possible merger between Lindsay Machinery and Douglas Enterprises. Rumor has it that Douglas is just waiting for you to fall flat on your face so that he can sweep up the rubbish."

Erin sucked in her breath, but still she maintained a steel control over her reaction. "I wouldn't have turned in the bid," she slowly replied, "if I had thought my company was not solvent enough to meet the cost, the deadlines, and the quality I promised."

"I'm sure of that," Raymond affirmed, his hand moving across the table to lie on hers. "I wouldn't have represented you otherwise. But Julio Cortez is not. The only way I could protect your interest and give you a chance at the contract was to agree to this open bidding."

"Open bidding!" Erin muttered ferociously. "And worse, open bidding with that man!"

Wisely Raymond leaned back in his chair and ordered himself another drink, waiting until Erin had cooled down, letting her cogitate, letting her mull. "The more you think about it," he finally allowed, "the more you'll realize that it's our only choice."

"The more I think about it," she asserted calmly, "the less unsavory I find the idea." Interest began to flame in her eyes. "Given time, I might even find it exciting." She sat for a few more seconds, thinking, then asked, "Why today?"

"Because Cortez is in Houston for the week, and he called to inform me this morning that he was in favor of awarding the contract to Devlin. I asked him to give you a chance to explain your bid in person. That's when he suggested the open bidding, and I agreed."

Erin took a long sip of her wine, relishing the sharp dryness. She ought to be grateful to Raymond, she thought. God only knew how badly she needed this contract. She set her glass on the table and ran her fingers around the base, considering all that Raymond had told her, digesting the full implication of all his words, weighing the importance of her actions.

"And if you want the chance," Raymond continued in that soft, persuasive voice, "it'll have to be today. You see," he added, "Devlin definitely has Cortez's ear."

She would have to take the chance, she decided, because she needed and wanted this contract. Rumor was right. Joseph Gerard Lindsay, chairman of the board for Lindsay Machinery, wanted to merge with Douglas Enterprises. But if and when she were forced to lead her company in a merger, Erin determined that it would be on her terms not Devlin's. Securing this contract would place her in an excellent bargaining position. So she had no choice but to speak with Julio Cortez.

"Well, Erin?" Raymond asked, having allowed her a moment of introspection. "What's it going to be?"

"You know what it's going to be," she snapped. "I want that contract, and I mean to get it."

"That's my girl!" Raymond praised her.

"Where are we meeting?"

"Here," he answered. "We're to meet Julio, his daughter, Alma, and Devlin in one of the private dining rooms."

Erin leaned back in her chair, lifting her brows and murmuring softly, "And just how old is Alma?"

He grinned. "Twenty-five and single. Beautiful too. Just my type."

"I think I can understand why Devlin has Cortez's ear," Erin muttered. "He probably has Alma's body."

Raymond chuckled. "Your claws are showing, my dear, and that's not good for Lindsay Machinery. Put your personal animosities aside and concentrate on the bid. Show Cortez how well Erin Lindsay conducts herself at the bargaining table." He smiled, giving her hand one last reassuring pat. "Cortez is no fool, and he respects good, sound business judgment." He stood. "And, furthermore, from what I've gathered Alma and Devlin have nothing going between them. He's a workaholic and has been ever since his wife died." He looked at his watch. "Time to go and show them the stuff that you're made of, Erin."

Erin smiled, pushing herself to her feet, glad that no one could see the stuff that she was made of. If they could have, they would have seen one gelatinous mass that was slowly melting to nothing. But as usual, Erin pushed her doubts and fears aside to stand proudly; she picked up her purse, dropped the black leather strap over her shoulder, and tucked the portfolio under her elbow.

"I'm ready whenever you are." She looped her arm through his, walking across the lounge, into the lobby, down the corridor, to a small but private dining room.

Raymond opened the door, and Erin stepped in ahead of him, her head high, her face set in determined resolve, a flinty gleam in her eyes. With that straightforward gaze of hers, she quickly surveyed the small group that was seated around the table. The older man she judged to be

Julio Cortez. The woman, Alma. The third man, Devlin Douglas himself!

While Raymond made the introductions, and as they all murmured their urbane replies, Erin took the time to study her competitor. In his mid-forties, she thought, remembering a recent article about him. And although he couldn't be called handsome, he was certainly distinguished. Impeccably dressed, his thick black hair was winged to the side, burnished and shining, contrasting with the stark whiteness of his shirt. His ebony eyes reflected the darkness of his three-piece suit, and amusement swirled as vividly in his eyes as the red, black, and gray stripes spiraled in his tie.

"Hello, Erin," Devlin said as if they were old acquaintances on the best of terms, "I'm glad to see you here."

"Thank you, Mr. Douglas," she grated softly between clenched teeth, watching and feeling those ebony eyes as they flickered over her, not missing one small detail.

Not bad, he thought, liking the soft hair that was pulled back in that cluster of curls. Very demure and sedate. Probably done on purpose to make her look older than her thirty-odd years.

Aware that she amused Devlin, Erin grudgingly allowed him to seat her and quickly turned her attention to Julio and Alma. Throughout the delicious meal, the five of them indulged in desultory conversation, discussing the renovation of the dairy and its subsequent conversion into one of Houston's most popular restaurants. All of them hid their preoccupation with the bidding behind the mask of politeness, half-listening to the small talk, indifferently answering questions and making comments. All the while the cogs of their brains were silently practicing and rehearsing more serious concerns.

"Now," Julio finally announced when all had finished their desserts and he was lighting his cigar, "if it pleases you, Erin—" he turned his head first at her and smiled charmingly; then he looked at Devlin "—and if it pleases you, Devlin, we'll turn our attention to business matters." Both of them nodded their assent.

On cue Alma rose, smiling down at her father. "If Mr. DeLaGarza doesn't mind, Poppa, I'd like to go through the museum and the spring house."

Quite happily Raymond rose, vociferously exclaiming, "Not at all. I'll be more than happy to take you. The museum is fantastic, and the spring house is out of this world."

When the two of them were gone and when the door had been closed, a sudden hush descended on the three who were left. Julio puffed on his cigar for a while before he asked, "Would you care for something to drink?"

"A glass of iced tea, please," Erin requested.

"Coffee," Devlin stated.

"And I'll have coffee too," Julio pronounced.

Quickly he gave the command and in seconds the dairymaid had scurried out to get the drinks. While Erin and Devlin sugared their tea and coffee, Julio lifted his attaché case and extracted two manila folders, placing them in front of him. Then he picked up two envelopes, handed one to Erin, and the other to Devlin.

"I'll keep the original bid that each of you submitted to me, but for your convenience I made one photocopy of each that I'm giving to you. If you'll turn through your copy, you'll find sections and items marked by either Hernandez or myself. In the margin we wrote our comments and questions." He leaned back, lifting his cup to his lips. "Please, take all the time you need to read the notations."

Closely he watched Devlin and Erin as they opened their package. He had to admire their poise and aplomb. Neither gave any indication of being nervous. Worthy opponents, he decided, and he was sorry that he couldn't give both of them the contract. And at this precise moment he wondered which one would win the bid. At first he had been sure that it would be Devlin, but since he'd met Erin, he had doubts. Already she had impressed him.

Slowly the minutes ticked by, only the turning of the pages breaking the silence. Erin meticulously studied the annotated copy of her bid, jotting comments on it herself, her sharp mind working in high gear. And although she had determined to fight to the bitter end, she wondered if she really stood a chance. She had the feeling that Devlin had already underbid her. He could afford to. This contract wasn't as important to him as it was to her.

When she finally raised her head, dropping her pen on the table, both Julio and Devlin were watching her. It was unnerving, but she didn't allow her uneasiness to show. She smiled, lifting her glass to her lips, thankful for the cool, refreshing flow that soothed her parched throat.

"Ready?" Julio asked, his eyes darting from Erin to Devlin. When both nodded, he leaned forward, adjusting his glasses on his face. "As you know, I can't give the contract to both of you." Since it was a statement that demanded no answer, neither spoke. "As for me, I was favoring Devlin's bid, but Adolfo leans toward your bid, Erin." Now he paused, looking at her, waiting for her reply.

"Since you're admitting that you favor Devlin's bid, and since Adolfo isn't here to lend me support," Erin asked quietly, "are you going to listen impartially to what I have to say?"

"I am," Julio averred softly. "I wouldn't have consented to Raymond's suggestion of meeting with you if I hadn't had some reservations about my choice." He sighed. "I cannot afford to make a mistake. Too much depends on my decision."

Nodding, believing the sincerity of his words, Erin took a deep breath and began to talk. "In section one, item three, my figures are high, but they are not outrageous when you consider the quality of materials with which I'm working or the quality of the finished tool that I'll be giving you. Nor are the figures high, Mr. Cortez, when you consider the written guarantee." She lowered her head, running her finger down the sheet of paper. "If you'll just follow, I'd like to explain this to you." Very quickly she read the warranty aloud, explaining it clause by clause. Then she said as she opened her portfolio, pulling out several sheets of paper, "If you'll look these over, you can see all the raw materials that go into our finished product." She leaned over the table, tracing the left side of the paper with the blunt end of her pen. "This column is our cost for the raw materials." Her pen glided across the page. "This is the cost of the finished tool."

Leaning forward, snapping the cap from her pen, she looked at the annotations she had made, and with a calmness that came with her strong faith in Lindsay Machinery, Erin launched into a detailed but succinct explanation of her bid. At another point she again opened her portfolio, pulling out her research papers, showing Julio the results of her study and subsequent planning.

"As you can see, Mr. Cortez, Lindsay Machinery specializes in farm equipment, and we're accustomed to large-volume orders. We're small but efficient, and we produce quality products. Also we are willing to put our maintenance warranties in writing, a standard practice for us, but a policy that most of our leading competitors do not follow." At this point she could feel Devlin's eyes bearing down on her, but she refused to glance his way even for an instant. Continuing with her presentation, she said, "True, our cost may be higher, but remember my quality is also superior and our work guaranteed."

Having listened patiently, Devlin felt that it was his turn to speak. "May I now point out," he interrupted smoothly in a deeply resonant voice, his ebony eyes still laughing at Erin, "just because you're small and because you specialize in farm tools does not necessarily guarantee a better deal. In fact, Julio, I would say that the size of Erin's company would be one great disadvantage of her entire package." His eyes moved from Erin's face to Julio's. With an arrogant calmness that infuriated Erin, he began an eloquent defense of his bid which smirked of a deliberate rebuttal of Erin's explanation. As he spoke he easily refuted all the points she had made, one by one, missing none.

All the while Erin carefully listened, and she wrote. Yet she kept a tight rein on her expression and on her actions. She knew that so far she had impressed Julio, and she knew that she had a chance, a slim one, but nonetheless a chance. She must govern all her actions with care and thought. She must move slowly and easily.

"I can understand your line of reasoning," Erin argued softly when Devlin had concluded, "but more clearly I believe I can see what you're not offering in your bid, Mr. Douglas." Those blue eyes icily surveyed Devlin. "Mr. Cortez," she addressed him, "will you please turn to section three, items five, seven, and eight." As she talked, she flipped the pages of her copy, circling all the items she had enumerated. "So far, Mr. Douglas has made no mention of these provisions." She waited for Julio to read the designated clauses, and she glared at Devlin, triumph glowing in the cool depth of those blue eyes. "To my knowledge Lindsay Machinery is the only manufacturer still making these guarantees at this cost."

"Hmmm," Julio droned, studying the bid in front of him. "This is probably the most attractive aspect of your bid," he admitted. Looking up, addressing Devlin, he said, "Well, Devlin, what have you got to say?"

He popped question after question at Devlin, waiting for the answers which were slow in coming at times. As Devlin sat there, his brow furrowed, his eyes lowered, he studied the mounds of papers in front of him, wondering if he had misjudged Erin Lindsay. And he was furious when Julio chuckled softly at his inability to answer a question.

The first hour passed, the second began, and the tension slowly mounted higher and higher. Erin requested another glass of tea, Devlin another cup of coffee. Other than this, they never betrayed their tension. But as time went by, Devlin carefully pushed Erin into a corner, letting his bid drop even lower than what it already was.

Erin listened to Devlin, and she heard Raymond's words reverberating through her mind. Should she lower her bid, she wondered. It's worth whatever she would have to do to get it, she thought. But even now her figures allowed her hardly a margin of profit. Yet if she got this contract, it would guarantee her other Latin American contracts.

Desperately clinging to Raymond's words, Erin uttered a lower bid, looking at Devlin. "Can you better that one?"

Returning the smile, his eyes ribald with laughter, Devlin never replied. He simply stood and walked around the table, seemingly in need of stretching his legs.

"Well, Devlin?" Julio softly demanded, "can you?"

Without turning, and with a nonchalance that made Erin seethe, Devlin quoted an even lower figure. When the silence became too heavy for him to endure any longer, he turned, a look of triumph gleaming in his eyes. *Dare you go any lower than this, Erin?* he seemed to be saying.

Erin met his gaze steadily, calling a new bid. She regarded Devlin with cold, hard eyes that directly contrasted with the soft huskiness of her voice.

Devlin chuckled, lifting the cup in salute. "Well, Erin, it seems that you've underbid me. I could go lower, but I think this is as low as I want to go. I think I've accomplished my purpose in coming." Letting the words fall where they would, he walked back to the table and began to shuffle his papers together. "Julio, this is it." He picked up several sheets of paper, hastily writing on them. After he had stuffed them into the envelope, he tossed the package to the older man. "I'm not prepared to go any lower. Make your decision based on these last figures."

Pleased with the proceedings, Julio nodded his head, holding his hand out for Erin's sheets. He smiled. "I don't see how I can afford to refuse Erin's bid," he mused. "It is truly an extraordinary one." He looked across the table at her. "Are you sure that you can deliver?"

"I'm sure," she returned, never flinching from his direct gaze.

"I wonder," Devlin faintly scoffed, adding louder so that Julio could hear him, "If she can't, you can always contact Douglas Enterprises. But remember this, Julio Cortez, you'll never get this offer again."

Julio chuckled. "The words of the vanquished."

Erin snickered, and even Devlin's face crinkled with laughter, his eyes swirling with secret amusement. If he had calculated correctly, he had pulled Erin's bid so low that she couldn't afford to meet the terms of the contract. And, if this were true, she would soon be ready to discuss a merger.

"No, Julio," he softly negated, "not the words of the vanquished. The joyous cry of the victor."

Devlin's words weren't really for Julio at all; they were addressed to Erin, and she understood their full implication. She could almost read his mind, but she ignored him, continuing to gather her things together. All the while, however, she was castigating herself for her foolishness. Why had she listened to Raymond? How could she have allowed herself to bid this low! She, Erin Lindsay, reputed to be a level-headed businesswoman, had let this man lead her to a trap into which she had willingly jumped and locked herself.

The irony of the situation struck her when she shook hands with Julio, thanking him for the contract. She watched him as he walked out of the room in search of Alma and Raymond; then she slowly picked up her purse, fishing for her car keys before she slung it over her shoulder.

"Congratulations seem to be in order," Devlin announced, walking nearer to her. "May I congratulate you, Erin?"

She smiled brilliantly, throwing her head back in that last act of defiance. "You may, Mr. Douglas, and you may also do me one other favor!"

He lifted his brows, his sensuous lips curving into a large friendly smile. "And what's that, Erin Lindsay?"

"Don't call me Erin. That's a privilege reserved only for my friends."

The smile remained on Devlin's face, but the soft amusement that had been lurking in the depths of his eyes was wiped away to be replaced with sardonic mockery. He stared at her until she thought she could stand it no longer, but she never twitched a muscle. She forced a smile, and she lowered her eyes.

"Are you always this discourteous?" he asked with an odd gentleness.

"Not always," she retorted coolly, drawing up to her full height. "Only when I'm dealing with someone who warrants such treatment."

"What makes you think I warrant it?"

She lifted a hand, her fingers playing with the beads at her throat. "I've heard about your ruthlessness, and I know what you've done since you've extended your operation into Houston, Mr. Douglas. Would it suffice to say that I know what you did to Sheldon Temple and Claude Barrington?"

"And based on what you've heard," Devlin accused her, "you've already judged and condemned me. You really disappoint me, Ms. Lindsay. I had expected more from you, but—" he shook his head "—I guess I expected too much."

"Or too little," Erin rebutted effectively.

Devlin grinned at her comeback. "Not too little, Erin Lindsay. I've had the pleasure of hearing about you firsthand. Your father told me that you were one helluva businesswoman, one tough lady."

"He's right," she conceded easily. "And he ought to know. He was my personal instructor in the school of hard knocks."

Joe G. had taught her to be tough. He had seen to it that she learned to sacrifice everything. How hard the lesson had been at the time, but she had learned. "Tears," Joe G. had said, "were a waste of time, energy, and emotion. They changed nothing." And how quickly Erin learned this lesson.

How well she remembered her first love, her first fiancé but not her first lover. Joe G. had burst into her life after her mother died and bought Jeremy off before their relationship had gone far enough for him to become her lover. For a paltry sum of money Jeremy Patterson had jilted her, not quite at the altar, but near enough.

And when he had walked out on her without so much as a good-bye, she had cried. For days she cried for what might have been. But she learned her lesson. No more tears after that, no more tears ever. She had spent the next few years of her life developing that callous indifference that shielded her from hurt and pain.

"You know," Devlin reflected, "I think, for a woman at the bargaining table, Erin Lindsay, you're pretty good."

"At the bargaining table, period, Mr. Douglas," Erin softly refuted, "I'm better than pretty good. I'm excellent."

"I wouldn't go that far," Devlin grinned, admiring her spirit and spunk. "You've done all right up to now, but today was your Waterloo."

Erin forced herself to laugh. "I hardly think so. I label today as a special victory."

He shook his head, dropping his hand to his hips. "Why did you react so foolishly?"

"I'm not sure that I follow your meaning?" Erin rebutted.

"Of course, you do! You let your dislike of me influence your bidding. You actually jeopardized your company by bidding so low, by erasing your margin of profits." Softly he taunted her, "You behaved very foolishly, Ms. Lindsay."

His smugness and his overly emphasized repetition of her name were having their effect on Erin. They grated on her frayed nerves, but with no show of her anxiety or her irritation, she spoke. "No," she stated in a saccharin-sweet voice. "I didn't jeopardize my company. I went for a contract, and I got the contract."

"At what price?"

"I paid a high price," she admitted, "but not too high." Recalling a fond memory of a person who had greatly influenced her life, Erin said, "One of my teachers in school, Mr. Douglas, Sister Anna Maria, often quoted an old proverb which I believe. No price is too high if you want something badly enough, and I wanted this contract badly enough."

"At the risk of losing Lindsay Machinery?"

"At the risk of saving Lindsay Machinery!"

"I can offer you a better way to save your company."

"Can you?" she murmured. "Just what is your solution?"

She knew what his answer was, but still she asked. Ever since she'd returned from Europe three weeks ago, he'd been trying to meet with her, but she had refused. Now she was glad. This man was more, much more, that she had anticipated.

"I think you know what my solution is."

"Having gotten rid of Temple and Barrington," Erin goaded, "you're now aiming for Erin Lindsay."

"Well, to be honest, before today I had been thinking only in terms of the company, but now that I've seen you in action, I am definitely interested in the woman as well as her company."

"I'm not joking," she shot back.

"Nor am I," he returned. "I've never been more serious in my life. I feel that you and I could work together very well."

"If I have my information correct, Mr. Douglas, you don't want to work with people. You either buy them out or run them into the ground."

"If I run people out of business," he retaliated with granite hardness, "then perhaps they shouldn't have been in business in the first place. But, may I point out, Ms. Lindsay, a merger is no disgrace. And it will be advantageous to both of us."

"Especially to Douglas Enterprises."

"No," he calmly refuted, "for the two of us."

"That's an opinionated statement," she threw back hotly, "and one that I don't agree with."

"Your father's already faced the inevitable, Ms. Lindsay," he stated flatly, not letting her rile his anger. "Why can't you?"

"He doesn't believe in Lindsay Machinery anymore," Erin replied stoutly. "I do. Therefore, Mr. Douglas, I'm willing to fight to hell and back for my company."

Devlin laughed softly. "How dramatic!"

"Just truthful," she corrected. "Now, will you please leave me alone."

"Can't," he softly elucidated. "I've discovered that I'm not only interested in the merger of our companies, but I'm now very interested in you."

"And I see nothing further to discuss on either point." Erin instructed quietly.

He shrugged. "I think I'll have to change your mind."

Erin's eyes slowly raked over the large frame—down, then up—meticulously, not missing an inch. "It would take more than what you've got to offer to make me change my mind." She spun on her heels, walking toward the door.

Lithely Devlin moved in front of her, blocking her way. "Let's call a truce," he negotiated softly. "I didn't come here today to argue with you."

"Really!" Erin scathed skeptically.

"Really," he returned. "My primary purpose in coming was to meet you. Every other advance I made has failed, and this seemed to be an excellent opportunity." His face softened, and his eyes grew deeper. "Now I'm glad that I did. I like the legend behind Lindsay Machinery. I admire the woman who's managed to outwit me at every turn."

Despite her resolve to hate this man, a small flicker of laughter wormed its way into Erin's eyes, and she allowed her lips to curve into a smile. "Mr. Douglas, you're gloating because you think you've got my firm in the palm of your hand. And nothing would please you any better than to add me to your list of conquests." She shifted her portfolio from under one arm to the other. "But let me warn you, I've been boxed in before, and I've always managed to escape."

Devlin grinned. "As I see it, you have only one avenue of escape. Although I admire your valiant stand, you played against a stacked deck, and you lost."

"To quote Sister Anna Maria again," Erin said calmly, "where there's a will, there's a way." She smiled into his eyes, the resolve glinting in hers. "I believe that, Mr. Douglas."

"I admire your determination also," he lauded her. "In fact, I admire you, period." As he made the pronouncement, his eyes gently flowed over the soft curves of her breasts, her trim waist, rounded hips, and long legs.

"I don't think a truce will work for us," Erin returned, her body warming under his assessing gaze. "I'm determined to save my company, and I'll do whatever I must." Her eyes still glinted with strong resolve. "When and if I agree to a merger, Mr. Douglas, I shall be in a position to demand certain terms and concessions."

"I'm not sure that I fully understand what you're talking about," he told her, his eyes twinkling. "Would you mind explaining this to me over dinner tonight?"

"I think you understand me very well," she quipped, murmuring, "just as I think I understand you."

He grinned. "A very smart lady indeed!" He paused, that humorous glimmer in his eyes. "Then let's have dinner tonight so we can discuss calling a truce."

Erin felt his vibrant energy, and she felt his strength as it flowed from him to her. At the same time her strong, unflinching gaze assured him that she meant what she said. She wasn't afraid to fight. On the contrary, she was prepared to fight.

"An obtuse man indeed," she thrummed. "Deliberately obtuse!"

"Deliberately," he agreed unrepentantly. "I like you, and I want to know more about you."

Erin gave way to her laughter, soft musical intonations of her soul. "I've been warned about your reputation, Devlin Douglas," she retorted, unwittingly using his first name. "Don't think you're going to win me over with soft talk and flattery." She stepped back and looked fully into his face, unaware of her slip.

"Please, Ms. Lindsay," Devlin admonished with feigned shock and outrage, his eyes ribald with sparks of laughter. "You'd better call me Mr. Douglas until we're better acquainted. Only my friends are permitted to call me Devlin."

It was a second before Erin realized her mistake; then

she stared at him blankly. Finally she muttered on choked laughter, "Touché!"

"However, Ms. Lindsay," he continued, impish delight openly winging through those raven eyes, "I'm willing to go along with whatever you deem proper."

A full, warm smile played on Erin's lips. She could understand why women fell victim to Devlin's charm. He was definitely big and brawny, but he was surprisingly gentle. His very presence, his aura of masculinity, his rugged attraction, all emphasized his virility, making him a man of whom a woman is instantly aware and one to whom she is instantly attuned.

"I think perhaps we've known each other long enough to use first names," she replied, aware of the fire that smoldered in Devlin's eyes, knowing instinctively that it was capable of burning away the barrier that she had so painstakingly built.

"Thank you, Erin." The soft words touched Erin deeply. "Will you have dinner with me tonight?"

She chuckled softly, the tones echoes of mirth. Soft and husky, they smothered him with their sensuality. "You're a fast worker," she teased him. "I don't think we've been on first-name basis long enough for this."

"A man my age can't afford to be too slow," he came back. "When he sees something he wants, he's got to go for it." His eyes clearly broadcast the double meaning of his words. "Well?"

Erin shook her head. She wasn't ready for a man like Devlin Douglas to invade her life. "Not tonight."

"A pity," he told her. "You'd have a wonderful time."

"One man's opinion," she told him dismissively, stepping to the side.

"But the one I'm most interested in," he told her, stepping with her, still blocking her exit. "Lunch tomorrow?"

Again she shook her head. "Not dinner. Not lunch." She spoke softly. "I was telling you the truth, Devlin. I have no interest in playing games with you, business or otherwise."

Devlin smiled slowly, and delight twinkled in those deep black eyes. "Now, that statement is quite revealing." The gentle banter softly rubbed Erin's exposed nerves.

"Not really," she countered. "I just think you're trying a new tactic, one I'm not falling for."

"Somehow or other," he pondered aloud, "I don't think you've played enough games in your life, Erin. Maybe it's time for you to relax a little."

"I'm quite capable of taking care of myself," she retorted smoothly. "And, believe it or not, I maintain a healthy balance between work and relaxation." Her eyes glittered mischievously. "I'm just very selective about my playmates."

"Aren't you curious about me at all?" he questioned, reluctant to leave her. "Wouldn't you like to go out with me just to find out what makes me tick?"

Now Erin laughed. "I'm not a clockmaker," she quipped. "I have no desire to find out how or why you tick."

"Hard-hearted Hannah," he accused. "Or is it cold-hearted Erin?"

"Your choice," she bit out dryly, lifting her wrist to look at her watch, hoping that he would take the hint.

"You know, Erin Lindsay," he said, liking the feel of her name on his lips, "I believe that underneath all that camouflage of toughness and indifference, you are curious about me. I also believe," he went on, "that you're afraid to go out with me."

"Think what you will," Erin shot back, "I can't stop your thinking."

"Or wanting," he added on a faint whisper, "or hoping."

"Or wanting or hoping," she concurred.

"I like you, Erin. Give me a chance to prove it to you.

And give yourself a chance to like me." He lifted his lips in a lopsided grin. "I'm really a very likeable fellow."

Staring directly into his face, Erin said, "I don't like you, Devlin Douglas, and I don't think I ever will. Nor do I want to go out with you. I'm perfectly happy with my life just as it is. Now, if you'll please step aside," Erin enjoined heatedly, realizing that she'd never penetrate that thick skull of his, "I'll just be on my way. I do have work to do this afternoon."

He moved without another word, watching as she walked across the room, her black high-heeled pumps sinking into the thick pile of the carpet. "It's been nice meeting you, Erin. I wouldn't have missed this for the world."

Reaching the door, her hand on the knob, Erin turned, bestowing a final smirk of triumph in his direction. "It's been nice meeting you, too, Devlin, but it's been even nicer winning the bid out from under you."

"I can imagine," he rejoined dryly. "Be seeing you around."

"Not if I can help it," she quipped airily, spinning on her heel.

"I don't think you're going to be able to help it," Devlin retorted smugly, "unless, of course, you're not going to the trade fair next week."

Erin closed the door on his words, but they followed her down the corridor, laughing at her, mocking her, and reminding her that Devlin Douglas was the kind of man to have the last word at a woman's expense. Oh, well, she thought, taking a deep breath, she had won today, and she was optimistic about winning the next round. Surely the Cortez-Hernandez contract would pave the way for orders from other Latin American firms.

As the door banged behind Erin, Devlin walked to the deserted table and flipped shut the lid of his briefcase, folding his hand around the handle, dropping it to his side.

Although Erin seemed to be living up to the rumor that she was tough and cold, Devlin disagreed.

He would instead liken her to a magnum of fine wine that had been packed in ice, cool and delicious, but not for the faint of heart. The icy trappings were just a form of protection, and the hardened surface probably scared off lesser men who were fools to approach her in the first place. But he didn't scare that easily, nor did the appearance of things daunt him. In this instance, he thought with a smile, the appearance of things whetted his curiosity and interest. It made him want Erin Lindsay all the more, and what Devlin Douglas wanted he usually got.

CHAPTER TWO

Erin stood in front of the Lindsay Machinery booth at the Convention Center in San Antonio, hands on hips, making last-minute changes in her display. Her hair was casually pulled from her face and tied at the nape of her neck with a red ribbon, just one of the many colors that dotted her cotton shirt and one that matched her red slacks.

"Pull the *l* a little to the right," she called, shading her eyes with a hand so she could see better.

"How's this?" Raymond grunted from atop the ladder as he cautiously moved the letter.

"Too far," she shouted. "Back to the left. Hold it! That's good. Leave it right there."

"Make sure this is the way you want it," Raymond advised her shortly. "When I get down this time, I'm finished for the day. I'm hungry, and I'm ready to eat." He lowered himself on the ladder, mumbling, "I don't know why you hire people to design these sets and put them together if you're gonna redo it. Every trade fair that we attend, we redo the entire display."

Erin laughed good-naturedly, moving backward so she could see the booth better. "I like to feel that I've contributed something of myself to the display. You know, the personal touch."

"Right now I need a personal touch," Raymond grumbled. "I need nourishment."

"All you think about is food."

"Not quite," Raymond refuted. "I think about women too." He lowered himself another rung. "Well, do you think it's okay? I don't want to dangle from this ladder all day."

"It's beau—" Erin cut her sentence short when she bumped into someone. "Oops," she apologized, turning her head, saying, "I wasn't watching where I was—" Again she stopped in mid-sentence, the words sticking in her throat. "Devlin Douglas!" she whispered.

"Well! Well!" that all too familiar voice taunted softly, his arms wrapping around her. "What a wonderful surprise!"

"I'll bet," Erin snapped. "We didn't think you'd be here this early. We haven't seen your display."

Devlin chuckled. "At least you've been looking. Now, I take that as an indication that you didn't entirely forget me." His eyes raked over her work-soiled clothes, his smile turning into a teasing grin. "In fact, it seems that you're so happy to see me that you've thrown yourself into my arms."

"That'll be the day," Erin grunted, pushing herself away from him, her eyes appreciatively running his masculine length, liking the soft western shirt that was tucked into the waistband of the low-riding jeans. "It's your fault that I backed into you."

Devlin quirked his brows. "Oh?"

"You knew where you were going, and I didn't. So you could have avoided the collision."

"True," he murmured, those black eyes sensuously flowing honey over her, "but why should I? I like having you in my arms, Erin Lindsay. It feels good."

"Though completely unintentional on my part?" she sputtered indignantly.

"A resourceful man makes do with what he can get," he quipped, nonchalantly bending his arms, turning up his cuffs to reveal thickly muscled forearms.

"In case you've forgotten," Raymond interrupted sarcastically, "I'm still up here, and I'm not a bird who loves to perch. If you can take the time, I would appreciate an answer."

Neither Erin nor Devlin took their eyes off each other.

"Beautiful, Raymond," Devlin called. "Simply beautiful."

Irritated and touched, Erin spun on her heel, intending to put some distance between her and Devlin, but her tennis shoe caught on an untied lace, and she tottered, falling against him. Automatically his arms opened and closed around hers.

"Devlin Douglas," she lashed out furiously, "you did that on purpose!"

Devlin, taking advantage of her frustration, drew her nearer to his firm build. "I might be guilty of wanting to hold you, Erin, but I didn't untie your shoelaces." The ebony eyes swirled with gentle amusement.

"Of all the gall!" Erin fumed, pushing out of his arms.

"I just couldn't resist," he apologized lightly. "You know, the personal touch."

Having given up on receiving an answer from Erin, Raymond lowered himself to the floor and folded the ladder, tucking it under an arm. As he walked away, he said, "I'll see you in an hour, and don't be late if you want me to take you to Market Square."

"To the market or to the restaurant?" Erin teased.

"I'm taking you to El Mercado," Raymond elucidated. "I'm taking me to the restaurant for some of the best Mexican food in San Antonio." He moved toward Devlin, holding his hand up in the air, grinning. "I would shake, but as you can see, Erin's had me booth-cleaning and I'm filthy."

"But the display looks good," Devlin praised. "There's just something about a woman's loving touch."

Raymond chuckled as he walked away. "Yeah," he muttered, "there is, and we men just can't seem to do without it."

"We seem to crave it even when the woman doesn't appreciate us," Devlin added, turning back to Erin. Softly he asked, "Have you ever thought about treating me civilly like Raymond does?"

"No, I haven't," she retorted, wishing Devlin weren't so likable, wishing that he weren't so gentle with her. She picked up her things and stuffed them into a plastic bag. "Well, so long, Devlin. Be seeing you tomorrow, I guess."

"Leaving so soon?"

"So soon," she quipped. "You heard the man. He won't hesitate to leave me if I'm not ready."

"If he should leave you, I could always take his place."

"No, thanks," she rejoined with no second thought. "I've already made my plans, and I don't intend to be late; therefore, Raymond won't leave me." She grinned.

"A pity," he shrugged. "You don't know what fun you're gonna miss."

"As long as I don't know," Erin threw over her shoulder, scurrying away, "then I can't miss it, can I?"

Long after she was gone Devlin stood in front of the booth, her soft laughter haunting him, her illusive perfume tantalizing him. But she, without a backward glance, quickly moved down River Walk, enjoying the briskness of the November morning, looking forward to her leisurely afternoon at Market Square.

Wasting no time once she reached her hotel room, she showered and selected her clothes, slipping into her new winter-white slacks and matching tailored blouse. While she shrugged into her red loose-fitting jacket with three-quarter sleeves, she slid her feet into her mid-heel red sandals.

Nearly ready, she walked to the mirror and stood for the longest time, deb   g. Should she wear her hair up or loose? Finally her decision made, she compromised between the two extremes. Hurrying to her suitcase, she rummaged until she found her large mother-of-pearl barrette. Using this, she pulled her hair from her face and clasped it at the nape of her neck. Now for the tiny matching earrings, she thought. Just as she began putting them into her ears, she heard the taps on the door.

"Just a sec," she called, stepping back, looking in the mirror for that final check.

Pleased with her appearance, she picked up her purse and walked to the door, excitement and anticipation giving her a lovely, natural glow. She reached out and opened the door at the same time that she lowered her head, rifling through her purse for her key. "Sorry, I took so long," she apologized, "but I—" She broke off to mutter, "Oh, shoot! Where's my key?"

"Do you realize, Erin, that this is the second time today that you've apologized to me? This must be a record high for you!"

Her key forgotten, Erin's head shot up, and her eyes rounded like saucers. "You!" she hissed furiously, staring into Devlin's grinning face. "What are you doing here?"

"Well, it so happens that Raymond couldn't make it, and I did offer my services."

"I don't need them," she spat out.

He shrugged, turning away, walking down the corridor. "I was afraid you'd say that." He didn't stop until he pressed the elevator control.

"Wait a minute!" Erin shouted, running after him. "What happened to Raymond?"

"Not what," Devlin calmly corrected, taking her open purse from her unresisting hands, looking for her key with no break in his conversation, "but who." He held the key up.

Ungraciously Erin jerked her purse from him with one hand and her key with the other. "Who?" she grated.

The doors of the elevator swished open, and Devlin stepped inside. "If you want to find out," he advised her, "you'll have to ride down with me." He caught Erin by the wrist and pulled her inside before the doors glided together.

"Well," she adamantly demanded, "who?"

"Alma Cortez." Devlin's lips tipped into that lopsided grin. "Seems that she's more appreciative of Raymond's virtues than you are."

"And that being?"

"She loves to cook, and collecting recipes is her hobby. When Raymond learned this, he couldn't resist her charms. So he went to the airport to pick her up."

"And I don't suppose that you were the one to point out Alma's virtues to Raymond, were you!" she pelted, following Devlin out of the elevator across the lobby.

He didn't answer until after he had given the valet his key and had asked for his car. "Erin, how could you!" he chided innocently. "Raymond was in a dilemma, and I had the solution."

"As usual," Erin grumbled, "you've got the answer."

"Not always," he returned with mock modesty. "But today I did. Raymond made no secret of wanting to go to the airport to pick up Alma, and I made no secret of wanting to shop at El Mercado."

"I'll bet you wanted to go shopping," Erin snorted.

"Erin, your disbelief in me is painful," he alleged, holding his hand over his heart. "How can you be so cruel?"

"Just runs in the family," she retorted dryly.

"This way," he pointed out, "no one will be disappointed. I'll take you to El Mercado, and the four of us will meet later for dinner."

"No way," Erin ground out.

"Well," he said, "if that's your final word, I'll accept it, but . . ." He lowered his head, his voice trailing into a pensive quietness. "I wonder how Raymond and Alma will feel when you don't show up? Just think how hard Raymond worked on that contract for you! Think what Alma will tell her father! Such ingratitude!"

"Blackmail," Erin accused softly, a smile creeping steadily across her face. "You're stooping to blackmail!"

"You're right, Erin," he conceded easily. "I'll stoop to almost anything to be with you. How about it? We'll be in the most public places of all San Antonio." The ebony eyes were cajoling in their brilliance. "Can't you spare a lonely man this much?"

"Well," Erin allowed, "I did have my heart set on seeing El Mercado."

"Then be my guest," Devlin said, leading her to his car. "Be my girl for the day."

"Your guest but not your girl," she corrected as he opened her door. And nothing more than general remarks were made as Devlin quickly drove the car across the downtown area, parking in the elevated lot above the farmer's produce market. But he didn't immediately move to get out of the car, rather, he turned on the seat and looked at Erin.

"You look nice."

"Thanks," she murmured. A sudden apprehensive chill ran down her spine, causing her to shiver, which did not escape Devlin's notice.

"Are you cold?" he asked.

"It's nothing," she told him.

"Come closer to me, and I'll keep you warm."

She smiled, shaking her head. "No, thanks. I'll get warm as soon as we get out and walk around in the sunshine."

Devlin's laughter filled the car, totally engulfing her

with his sensuality, making her far too aware of him as a man. "But not nearly as exciting as my warming you."

"But safer," she countered.

"Probably is," he agreed solemnly, his lips twitching into a whimsical smile. "But you wouldn't be where you are today if you'd always played it safe, Erin." When she glowered at him, he chuckled. "Let's forget all our preconceived ideas about each other. Let's forget that you and I are competitors." His earnestness and his tenderness soothed and persuaded Erin at the same time. "Let's pretend that we like each other and that we want to know each other better." His hand swept across the seat, closing around hers, his grip sure and firm.

Erin, however, pulled her hand from his clasp and struggled to free herself from the web of enchantment in which Devlin was successfully entangling the two of them. Slowly she spoke. "If that's the way you get your kicks, then have at it. But I don't want to pretend. That's not for me." She reached up and ran her hand under her hair, cupping the nape of her neck. "I'll go to the market with you because I want to and because I'll enjoy it. But I'm not going to be part of your silly little games."

Even as Erin uttered the words, though, she knew she was trying to convince herself as much as Devlin. During the past week she had thought of Devlin many times. She hadn't been able to get those dark eyes out of her mind; she couldn't forget that endearing but maddening grin. In spite of every precaution that she'd taken, Devlin Douglas had touched her that day at Quail Ridge Dairy Farm. Very definitely he had touched her. It was almost as if he had already branded her for his own.

But she wouldn't admit this to him, or to anyone, for that matter, because she refused to accept this uncanny feeling that she and Devlin were somehow meant for each other was anything more than a romantic fantasy. He had already shown her how domineering he could be. At thirty-five she had established her routine, her habits, and her life-style. Certainly she didn't want any of these disturbed by a demanding man like Devlin.

"Tell me, Erin," Devlin quietly asked. "Haven't you ever pretended? Just for the fun of it?"

Not waiting for an answer, he opened the door, swung his legs out, and in a pronounced silence he escorted her down the stairs, and across the street into Market Square. "Take your choice," he said, sweeping his hand around the large square. "You lead, and I'll follow."

From the moment they entered El Mercado, Erin felt as if she had stepped back in time and as if she had been transported to Old San Antonio. She moved from shop to shop, looking at the beautiful imports, admiring the brightly colored hand-embroidered Mexican dresses. For the better part of two hours, with Devlin faithfully following behind, Erin meandered through the building as she made her purchases.

"Through here?" Devlin asked when they had made the full circle.

"Umm-hmm," Erin nodded, moving through the door that he held open, blinking as her eyes grew accustomed to the bright sunlight. "Don't you feel as if we've stepped back into time?" she asked.

Devlin pulled a face. "My, my! This doesn't sound like the Erin Lindsay I know. Is there a little of the romantic in you after all?"

Erin laughed. "No, but Market Square is authentically Old San Antonio." She moved across the courtyard. "Just look at these old buildings that have been renovated and turned into stores, and restaurants, and—"

As they passed the street café, he asked, "Are you ready for lunch?"

Erin started to shake her head; then she began to laugh. "You know, I am hungry. But," she hastened to add, "if we're going to have Mexican food tonight, I want to save some room for that."

"We have plenty of time to work off the lunch," he promised, guiding her toward the hostess. "When we get through eating, you can finish your shopping here in the market, and then we'll do some sight-seeing. We'll ride one of the Via trolleys around town, and we'll stop off at the Governor's Palace. By the time we walk back here, you'll be thirsty and hungry all over again."

In a few minutes they were seated at a small table for two, their lunch ordered, their drinks in front of them. "You're quite familiar with San Antonio," Erin commented curiously.

He nodded, leaning over the table, crossing his arms, resting his weight on them. "I spent a lot of time here when I was growing up."

Surprised, Erin asked, "You lived in San Antonio when you were a child?"

"Nope," he answered. "Seguin. But I came here often enough." He took a long drink of his beer. When he set his glass down, he asked, "Where did you spend your childhood?"

"New Orleans."

"Cajun?" he asked.

"Half," she returned. "On my mother's side." Her eyes lit up as she recalled memories of her childhood and her mother.

"I wonder what you were like as a child," he mused, his eyes moving over her countenance. And again he repeated, "What were you like, Erin?"

She shrugged self-consciously, sipping her drink. "A pretty ordinary little girl I suppose. What about you?" She avoided further discussion about herself.

"There's not much to tell about myself," he returned with a smile that tugged at Erin's heartstrings.

"Then it won't take you long to tell me."

"I was educated mostly through the school of hard knocks," he replied.

"No formal education at all?" Erin asked skeptically.

"A little," he admitted, downing another swallow of his beer. "High school in Seguin and bachelor's degree from Texas Lutheran."

"I see, Mr. Douglas," she mocked gently, "that you have a propensity to exaggerate and to promote this myth about your crude, unpolished ways."

"It seems to have helped some, Ms. Lindsay. People treat me with a little more caution when they think I'm liable to react in some primitive, uncivilized manner."

"Now I know differently," Erin gibed.

"I should have known that sooner or later a beautiful woman would come along to discover the truth and perhaps use it against me." The ardor that permeated his dark irises heated the latent sensuality in Erin.

"I'm no Delilah," she protested, sitting for a few minutes in the silence, twirling the straw in her drink. "What else?" she eventually asked.

"I had a lovely marriage with Nancy Holloway for fifteen years before she died of cancer."

Not because she was callous and uncaring, but because she did understand, Erin didn't waste her time or his on the usual but empty, "I'm so sorry," or "I didn't know." Rather she said, "When?"

"About five years ago."

"You loved her very much."

"I did," Devlin softly averred. "And she loved me as much. We never thought about our happiness ending so quickly."

"Children?" Erin asked.

"Two beautiful girls."

"Who are?"

"Devalind and Nanette." His face glowed with that

certain pride that comes with being a parent. "A twelve-and an eight-year-old."

"And exactly how old are you?" Erin asked curiously.

His lips twitched humorously. "I'm forty-two. Exactly how old are you?"

"Thirty-five," she returned succinctly, not ashamed of her age.

"Now what?"

"What are the girls like?"

"Like other children their age," he returned, grinning. "They have dark hair like me, but eyes like their mother." His voice changed to a softness that Erin had never heard before. "Nancy had such beautiful eyes. Her most outstanding feature."

Erin felt a twinge of jealousy as she listened to him compliment his wife. And she hurt badly because she would never experience the joy of motherhood. She couldn't deny that she was even a bit jealous because Nancy had shared a most intimate relationship with Devlin, that of bearing his children. And she, Erin Lindsay, would never share that intimacy with any man.

"Where do the girls live?"

"With me. Where else?" He was definitely amused.

"Where are they now?"

"At home, going to school."

"Who are they staying with?"

"Mrs. Hooper, my live-in housekeeper." He smiled. "Anything else you'd like to know?"

"Do your parents still live in Seguin?"

"They do. On a small farm on the outskirts of town."

"Any brothers or sisters."

"Two brothers, Robert and Nathaniel. Two sisters, Patricia and Shirley. All younger than me. And out of the five only one lives in Seguin. Shirley."

The conversation lulled when the waiter served their

lunch, but after the first few bites Devlin renewed the topic. "Now it's your turn."

Taking her fork, Erin chased her food around the plate as she began to talk. "I'm an only child and the product of a broken marriage. When I was a baby, Joe G. and Mother separated, but they never got a divorce. Mother, a strict Catholic and very religious, didn't believe in them, and Joe G. wanted the protection of marriage but not the responsibility."

"Do I detect bitterness?"

"To put it kindly," she returned shortly, "one may call it bitterness. To put it truthfully, I'll call it hatred." She lifted her glass, taking a swallow of her drink. She didn't mind Devlin's knowing how she felt about her father. The sooner he knew, the sooner he would learn that Joseph Gerard Lindsay wouldn't sway her opinion about the merger one iota. "Instead of giving my mother the love she needed, he gave her empty promises and a broken heart. Instead of being a father to me when I needed him, he sent me money and continued to carve out a financial empire." Erin's voice had changed from a musical huskiness to a cold hardness. "Are you sure you want to hear more?" she asked. "My story isn't a happy one."

"I want to hear all you'll tell me."

"After I graduated from high school, my mother died, and I became engaged to Jeremy Patterson."

"First boyfriend," he asked with the sharp sting of jealousy he didn't bother to hide.

She smiled. "My high school boyfriend. My first fiancé. But not my husband."

"Why?"

"Before we could be married, Joe G. came thundering into my life, wreaking havoc with it."

"Perhaps your father really cared for you," Devlin suggested. "Maybe he felt that with your mother dead you needed him."

"I doubt it," Erin snapped coolly, pushing her plate aside. "But no matter. Eighteen is too old to wake up one morning to find yourself motherless and father-more. And on top of that it was too much to find that my all-of-a-sudden father believed that money was the universal answer to all problems."

"How did Joe keep you and Jeremy what's-his-name from reaching the altar?"

"The minute Joe G. entered my life he decided that Jeremy was marrying me for my money."

"Was he?" Devlin asked, interested in everything about Erin, sincerely trying to find her soul.

"The classic question!" she mocked. "Was he? Yes, he was interested only in my money. He couldn't have cared less about the poor little rich girl. When Joe G. offered him a sizable sum to forget me, Jeremy took it and hit the road, never once looking back, never stopping to say good-bye." She shrugged. "Goes to show how stupid I was at eighteen. I was willing to follow my heart and my love to the end of the world. Money wasn't that important to me. But Jeremy was different. He didn't want to end up with just me and no money, which is what Joe G. promised if he married me."

"You would have lived to regret your marriage ultimately." Devlin said.

"Perhaps I would have," Erin conceded. "But marrying Jeremy was a decision I should have been allowed to make, or, at least, Joe G. should have used a little more parental wisdom in handling the situation."

"He did have good intentions though," Devlin pointed out. "And parenting is a tough job, Erin, for the best of us. All of us fail at times."

"But not all the time," she quipped shortly. "And his intentions weren't all that admirable."

"Look at it this way," Devlin said pragmatically, "your father did render you a great service."

"Did he?" she breathed scathingly. "I'm not so sure about that!"

"Did you love Jeremy?" he asked. "Or was it just a teenage crush?" When Erin just shrugged and didn't answer, Devlin spoke again. "Have I pried too deeply?"

"No," she replied quietly, opening a door to the inner coffer of her soul that had been sealed for seventeen years. "It's just something I haven't discussed with anyone before, and I had to think about it." She smiled, again touched by the gentleness of this powerful man. "And now I realize that it's not nearly so bad or as painful as I had thought." Still, she sat a moment before she said, "I only thought I loved Jeremy. After Mother died, I needed someone to lean on, and I thought he was strong. It wasn't really love; he represented security to me." She laughed softly to herself, reflecting aloud, "I hadn't really thought about it in years. I was so young, so full of foolish ideas and dreams."

"Were they that foolish?" Devlin asked.

"They were," Erin asserted. "In thinking back I can see just how much I was affected by the strict morality of Mother and Sister Anna Maria."

"You don't have to be ashamed of that."

"I'm not," she returned, grinning. "I'm just suddenly seeing the pieces to the puzzle. And I think I've found the missing one. I hated Joe G. because he squelched my romance before it had budded into an affair, before I had a chance to decide what I wanted from it. As a result, when Jeremy left, I didn't even have the memories of a lover left. . . . I had nothing."

Although Devlin felt her loneliness, her sorrow, and her bitterness, her confession thrilled him. "Which bothered you more? Jeremy's actions or Joe's?"

Erin lifted a hand and caressed a curl that wisped around her temple. "I'm not sure. I was angered by Joe G. and hurt by Jeremy. The two seemed to run together, creating one great anguish. And even though I did grow up a little, I childishly clung to a dream that one day Mr. Right would come along."

"And did he?"

"That's a subject I like to avoid altogether," Erin said quietly, almost too quietly. Her memories of Ralph Tarrance were best forgotten. They were humiliating as well as painful.

"Someone who still means something to you?" Devlin deliberately pursued the topic; the thought of her still caring so much about this man filled him with bitterness.

"No," Erin answered slowly, "he doesn't mean anything to me now." She didn't, however, add anything else to her statement.

"It might make you feel better to talk about him too," Devlin counseled.

"There's nothing to talk about!" The answer was emphatic.

"Must be," Devlin persisted, "or you wouldn't be so determined not to talk about him."

After only a moment's hesitation Erin asserted, "You're right. I did think there was something to Ralph, or I wouldn't have married him." More for something to do with her hands than because she was hungry, Erin picked up a piece of her roll and buttered it. "After Jeremy left, I returned to Houston with Joe G. and attended college. Afterward I decided to work with Lindsay Machinery, beginning as a mechanical engineer, working my way up. I had no time for play, but I didn't want to play. And I certainly didn't want to think seriously about a man."

"Yet you took time to play and to think seriously about Ralph," Devlin mused. "Somewhere in this strictly business-oriented life of yours, you had time to play a little bit."

Erin nodded. "Ralph was a mechanical engineer, too, and he was a terrific friend." Cradling the glass in her hands, she lowered her head. "And that's the way it should have stayed. But I was lonely, and he seemed to like me. I thought he had looked beyond Joe G.'s money and had seen me. Because I believed he was marrying me, Erin Lindsay and not Lindsay Machinery or Joe G.'s bank book, I married him."

"You just liked him, and you married him?" Devlin couldn't hide his incredulity.

Erin sipped her drink before she answered. "I had fallen passionately in love once, and that turned out to be a disaster. I knew what I felt for Ralph and believed I could have come to love him eventually. A love based on companionship and mutual respect. I wanted a home and a family very badly, and I thought he could give it to me. I thought we could make it. But after we married I learned that Joe G. had maneuvered the entire scene. He not only paid Ralph to marry me, but he paid him for a grandchild."

Devlin detected a particular note in Erin's voice when she mentioned a child. "But there were no grandchildren, were there, Erin?"

"No," she returned steadily, "there were no grandchildren." *And never will be,* she added silently, wishing she could cry about it, wishing she could purge herself of the bitterness and the hurt.

Devlin sensed there was more to the story than what she had recounted so far, but he also knew that he shouldn't push her to share too much with him too quickly. And although he wanted to know all there was to know about this woman; to uncover every nook and cranny of her past, he was selfish enough to want her to tell him of her own free will. He didn't want to have to press her for each little tidbit, each token of intimacy.

Continuing the thread of her thought, Erin said, "After Ralph I had absolutely nothing left. No faith. No hopes. No dreams. And I felt centuries old. But I had learned my final and most important lesson. Everyone does have his price. Joe G. had been right all along."

"Ended in divorce?"

"Yes." The word was abruptly final, cold, and emotionless.

"Maybe it was best that you had no children."

"Perhaps," she shrugged, her hand automatically settling on her stomach.

She remembered the night, just one in a long series, when Ralph had come home drunk, smeared with lipstick, the scent of whiskey and perfume clinging to his clothes. The one night too many. She had told him that she was suing for divorce. Although he had pleaded with her, she had adamantly refused to change her mind.

Then he had given vent to an uncontrollable anger that Erin had never seen before, yelling and finally trying to strike her. She had run from the bedroom, but he caught her on the landing of the stairs. Desperately she had screamed for help, twisting and fighting, finally freeing herself. He had reached for her again, and when she dodged him, her foot caught on the hem of her robe, causing her to fall down the stairs. Thankfully she succumbed to unconsciousness, not awakening until days later.

Her first question had been, "My baby?"

"I'm sorry," the doctor had tried to console her. "We were unable to save the child."

When she was stronger, the doctor had informed her that she would never be able to have another child, and at that moment she had never hated anyone more than she hated Ralph. Because of his drinking and anger, he had killed her child, the one thing she could have loved, who would have loved her in return.

"There's been no one in your life since Ralph?" Devlin asked, striving to keep his voice casual and friendly.

Shaking off the loneliness and grief that descended on

her when she thought about her baby, Erin said, "Don't be silly. Of course there have been other men in my life."

When she laughed so convincingly, Devlin realized that he was jealous of these unknown men. And when she so lightly referred to them, he tensed, his fingers tightening around the handle of his beer mug, a frown of displeasure furrowing his brow.

"Two losers in your life," he vociferated, startling her with the vehemence in his voice. "Just two, but they've ruined your life."

"No, I don't think so," Erin contradicted him. "My losses haven't been as great as yours."

Devlin stared at her for a moment. "What do you mean?"

"I didn't truly love either Jeremy or Ralph, so I haven't missed them." Her eyes filled with sympathy as she looked across the table at Devlin. "But you loved Nancy, and she loved you. The two of you had the girls."

"Nancy's death was one of the most devastating experiences of my life," he admitted. "God only knows how much it hurt, Erin. An essential part of me died with Nancy, I thought. But after the first year I realized that she and I had had fifteen beautiful and full years, more years than some people have in a lifetime. I pushed my sorrow and self-pity aside and began, with the girls' help, to create a new life for us."

"That's what I mean," Erin refuted him. "You lost someone who meant something to you. I didn't."

Devlin shook his head. "At the time they did mean something to you, and they've done you damage." *They have destroyed a beautiful part of you, Erin. They have caused you to retreat and to hide from life. On the other hand, Nancy's love has caused me to want to find it again, to live life to its fullest. It's given me faith in people and in love.* "Neither Jeremy nor Ralph were worthy of you, Erin, worthy of the love you wanted to share with them, so I'm not sorry that your relationships didn't work out. I'm sorry for the way that your past has changed you, has filled you with doubt and fear."

Erin shivered as the full implication of his words sunk in, and she wished that she hadn't opened herself to him; she wished that she hadn't confided in him. What could she have been thinking of? This man had a powerful effect on her, one she was just beginning to realize. Now she was angry with herself because she had willingly and deliberately burrowed into intimacy with Devlin. She had knowingly placed herself in a vulnerable position.

"Erin, let me prove to you that all men aren't like that." He laid his hand over hers, and the warmth was secure and strong. It promised so much. "Let me show you that all men aren't just out for what they can get, that some truly do want to give. With me it can be different."

"I know," she acknowledged, looking at his hand, seeing the fine shadow of dark hair on his fingers.

His promise frightened her. She wasn't afraid that he would make love to her; she knew better than that. She was afraid that he wouldn't make love to her, that he would concentrate on discovering her, winning her trust, making her believe all those dreams she had put aside so long ago. Before long he would see her willingly lay bare to him that part of her that she hid behind the barrier of indifference. She feared that he would explore, possibly exploit, all her emotions that she had so painstakingly hidden through the years, buried carefully under layer after layer of ice. He wouldn't be satisfied with the little that she would offer. He would want more.

Keeping her distance for a night or even a month would be easy enough, she knew. But could she hold out longer, she wondered. Would she want to hold out longer? Already she had to admit to the physical attraction she felt for Devlin, an attraction that for her was astounding in its intensity. She told herself that if she saw him more, the attraction would lessen, but in actuality the reverse was true. And he had sensed it that very first meeting. Already the idea of his being an excellent lover had passed through her mind. Psychologically she had weakened. How long before she physically capitulated?

Almost as if he were attuned to her thoughts, Devlin quietly promised, "I'm going to get close to you, Erin."

"No," she answered with the hint of a smile on her lips, but utter seriousness in her eyes. "I'm not going to let you."

"I'm not going to ask permission," he told her. "You've opened the door, and I'm going to walk right into your heart." His hand closed over hers, and he exerted the most gentle pressure. "Don't close me out, please."

Erin had been independent too long to be cajoled by his sweet murmurings and his tender audacity. She had been hurt too deeply to succumb to love talk, and to her this is exactly what she considered it—love talk. She knew and she understood men and their ulterior motives. They would say and do anything to get what they wanted. And she knew that Devlin Douglas wanted that merger.

She pulled her hand from his. "Your poetic ideas about walking into my heart probably have more to do with lying in my bed." She regarded him over the small table, shaking her head. "No, thanks. You're not welcome in either." Picking up her purse and packages, she asked, "Are you ready to leave?"

"Not really."

"I am," she said, standing. "I'm tired of all this talk. I want to see the town."

"Am I getting too close to the door for comfort?" he laughed as he slowly stood to his feet.

"No," she retaliated coolly, "you're beginning to bore me."

"Am I?" he scathed dryly, angrily wadding the bill in his fist.

As they walked across the plaza, Devlin lapsed into silence, and Erin made no attempt to speak. She resolved that she would enjoy her day with or without his help. If he wanted to pout, she would let him. She smiled as his gait lengthened, and she had to walk faster to keep up with him. Let him stew awhile, she thought. It would do his oversize ego some good.

Slowly as they rode the trolley bus through town, Devlin's humor returned, and he began to show her places of interest. However, he kept the conversation on a light plane, never touching on the personal. It was not until they reached the Governor's Palace that Erin was again cloaked with Devlin's warm intimacy. But it wasn't intentional on Devlin's part. Erin gave in to the romantic nostalgia of the past.

"Isn't it beautiful?" she murmured as they moved through the house on Military Plaza that had once housed the dignitaries who governed San Antonio de Bexar.

"I think it's one of the best preserved pieces of Mexican architecture," Devlin added, following her through the small chapel into the large dining hall. "The walls are thick enough to keep out the weather and animals and to be a fortress," he explained. "And did you notice the corner fireplaces? Beautiful works of art, functional, space-saving, and energy-saving."

"Oh, Devlin," Erin cried, walking into the kitchen. "Come look at the stove. To be so old, it looks so modern." She ran her fingers across the stove top, bending to peer into the area under the burners where the wood was placed. "Just think it was built into the house," she murmured. "And the shelves. Look at them."

"These early Spanish settlers brought the know-how," Devlin lauded, touching the native stone that had been set into the recessed walls and used for shelves. "And Texas furnished the raw materials."

Excitedly Erin darted from room to room, saving the

courtyard. At last, however, her exploration of the house complete, she walked out of the large family room across the tiled walkway to the old well.

"It's almost as if we were set back in time, isn't it? Almost as if we were in the sleepy little village of San Antonio."

Devlin grinned, catching her hand, leading her to the vine-covered dining hall. "I, the governor, and you, my wife," he continued, "walking in the cool of the afternoon in our private courtyard."

"I hadn't thought that," Erin told him, turning her head, looking into that face that was so serious.

"But I have," he retaliated. "As we walked through the bedrooms I wondered what it would be like to share one with you."

Erin tried to pull away from him, but he wouldn't turn her loose. "Don't start that again, Devlin."

"Why not?"

"First of all, I *don't* wonder what it would be like to share my bed with you, and I don't want to wonder."

"And you're lying," Devlin accused her smoothly without a change in his expression. "You are wondering what it would be like to be possessed by me, and you are wondering what it would be like to possess me."

"Still pretending," Erin taunted. "And in this case you're definitely wrong. I don't want a man in my life; I don't need one."

"Oh, yes, Erin, you do. You need love in your life, and you need it badly. Why not admit it? There's nothing wrong with it."

"Oh, shut up," Erin snapped, "and let's get out of here. You're ruining everything for me."

Hidden behind the large columns of the vine-covered soldiers' mess hall, Devlin jerked Erin, pulling her close to his hard, lithe frame. "Let me tell you something, Erin," he said in a low voice. "Everybody needs a little honest affection in his or her life, and you're no different from the rest of us." His lips quirked sensuously into a beautiful, sweet smile. "Underneath that cold exterior you're a warm, living person just like me. You're a woman begging for all the love that some man can give her."

His hand cupped her face, holding it still as his lips moved closer to hers. But she wouldn't allow him to kiss her. Quickly she dipped her face, trying to evade his touch. "Please, let me go," she hissed angrily. "People are bound to walk out here anytime."

"I know that," he informed her softly, letting his lips gently touch hers. "I'm not a starry-eyed teenager who can't wait, Erin. But I promise you this. I will make love to you."

"I'm not promising that I'll let you make love to me," she whispered defiantly, yanking her arm from his grip.

He moved slightly. "How do you propose to stop me? You're as receptive to my advances as I am to yours."

"I'm not aware that I made any advances," she countered.

"You have," he told her. "You've let me know in many ways that you want me."

"Why, Devlin?" she questioned quietly. "Why me?"

"Is that so unusual?"

"Why are you pushing me so fast?"

"I want to love you."

"I've told you," she almost screamed, "I don't have time for emotional attachments. I don't want any."

"I don't believe that. I think you're just afraid. Afraid to enjoy life. Afraid to get involved, to give of yourself." Softly he added, "Possibly afraid that you'll love me."

Drowning in the sensuous current, Erin desperately grasped for safety, finding it in anger and accusations. "I think that merger means quite a bit to you, and you'll do anything to get it."

"What an opinion you have of me!" he exclaimed in

dead calm, his fury running so deeply he had to stop and wait before he spoke again. "Well, let me tell you something," he breathed heatedly, "and mark it in your memory. I wouldn't do just anything for this merger. As unscrupulous as you want to believe me to be, I do have integrity and a code of honor. Maybe not much of either, but at least a shred of both."

Erin felt the lash of his anger, and she was suddenly afraid of him. "I'm sorry—" she began.

"Shut up." He cut her off sharply. "And listen to me. I want to get something straight real quick. God only knows I haven't been living a celibate life since Nancy died, but I've never had to resort to lying or blackmail to get a woman. Nor have I ever used sex as a business strategy."

He moved a step nearer, his body pressing hers against the white stucco colonnade. "Since Nancy's death there have been no serious involvements for me," he confessed in flinty, unyielding tones. "She and I were too deeply in love for me to immediately jump into another woman's bed, and it's taken me a long time to get over losing her."

"Devlin, please," Erin begged, but he didn't hear her.

"I wanted to die with her, Erin, but I couldn't and I didn't. I had two little girls who needed me more than ever. Two little girls who'd just lost their mother. I couldn't let them lose their father too. I knew that I'd never make up for Nancy, but I promised myself that I would be the best father that any kid could have. So," he pelted unmercifully, "for the past few years I've been giving all my love, all of myself, to the girls." He paused, staring at her, drawing a ragged breath. "Until recently, until I met you, I didn't think I'd ever want a serious relationship with a woman again." The dark eyes bored into hers.

"Devlin," Erin tried again, "I didn't mean—"

"Forget it," he commanded softly, his anger evaporating, a sudden gentleness coating his words. "You're not really to blame. I guess I am coming on too strongly, too quickly. You can't know how I feel about you. And it's only natural that you would be suspicious."

He eased away from her, but they didn't move from the courtyard. Rather, they stood for a long while just looking at each other, not speaking. It wasn't until other sightseers joined them that Devlin led Erin out of the house, talking in general, putting her at ease. All the while, however, he planned his capture and siege of her heart and soul. He knew now that he must move slowly and carefully, but he was prepared for a long battle. Anything worth having, he'd learned, was worth fighting and waiting for.

When they stood on Military Plaza in the late afternoon sunshine, Devlin said, "Come on. We'll walk back to Market Square to meet Raymond and Alma."

CHAPTER THREE

Dressed in jeans and, over them, an unbuttoned shirt that flapped loosely around his hips, Devlin stepped through the double sliding doors onto the wooden deck, carrying a saucer with several slices of buttered toast. Setting the dish on the table, he walked to the sideboard of native cedar and poured himself a cup of coffee.

"What a great way to end a trade conference," he exclaimed contentedly, leisurely walking around the deck, drinking his coffee. "Out here in the Texas wilderness. Only God knows where."

"We're in between San Antonio and Blanco," Erin informed him dryly from her reclining patio chair, never lifting her eyes from her book. "Closer to Blanco than San Antonio, and the river that you're looking at is the Guadalupe. God knows where we are, I know where we are, and you know where we are!"

"My, my," Devlin remarked, "but you're in a sweet mood today." He moved toward the round cedar table, slinging his legs over the bench. "Care for some of my toast? It'll probably make you feel more sociable."

"Thank you," Erin declined pertly. "I've already had breakfast."

"Didn't you rest well last night?" Devlin asked solicitously, crunching on the toast. When she looked up and glared at him, he murmured, "I don't guess you did. I can't understand why! There was nothing to disturb you. Nobody but you and Mother Nature. What sweet communion!"

Erin didn't bother to hide her disdain. "I didn't have a chance to commune with Mother Nature," she quietly told him. "You and Myra Webster were too busy insulting her with that noise you called singing."

"Once you and I are living together, Erin, I can see that my singing will have to be restricted to the shower." He shook his head, filling his mouth with another bite of bread. "You just don't appreciate talent when you hear it."

"Are you never serious?" Erin asked. "How do you get any business accomplished when you act so—" she shrugged her shoulders and lifted her hand in a bewildered gesture, searching for the right word "—so addlebrained all the time."

"Addlebrained," Devlin spewed. "Addlebrained! You can call me persistent, determined, resolved, but addlebrained!" He lifted the cup and took a long drink of the hot coffee. "Will I never convince you of my seriousness?" He stood and walked to the sideboard for a refill. "Care for a cup of this delicious coffee?"

"Think I will," Erin replied. "Just enough cream to color it, please."

"Best coffee you've ever had," Devlin said, filling her cup to the brim, adding the cream and stirring before he carried it to her. "Wasn't it nice of Myra to get up before daybreak to do this for us?"

"Myra is still sleeping," Erin retorted coolly, "and I'm the one who did this for me. You may drink it because I made enough to sober up the entire household, but it's my coffee."

"But I wasn't drunk," Devlin retaliated, mimicking her.

"Then pretend you were," Erin instructed. "At least that would give you some excuse for your ludicrous behavior last night."

"My behavior!" he exclaimed. "My behavior was beautiful in comparison to yours. You didn't do anything from the time you arrived but sit in the corner of the living room, sticking your nose in the air, judging everyone."

Not deigning to answer, Erin sipped her coffee and flipped the page of her book, pretending to read.

"Why did you come, Erin?" he asked. "If you don't like the Websters, and you don't like their sort of entertaining, why did you accept an invitation to their country home?"

"Business," she returned shortly, looking into his face, never batting an eye, no admission of remorse on her countenance. "Plain and simple, Devlin. I came to protect my business interests."

Stupefied, he stared at her for a long time before he walked to the edge of the deck and gazed at the lush green lawn that fronted the crystal clear river. "Just when I think I understand you," he reflected, "you show me a different facet of your personality."

Holding her cup in both hands, the rim close to her lips, Erin advised him in an equally quiet voice, "Don't try to understand me, Devlin. Just accept me for what I am. I'm not interested in your delving into who I am."

He sat on the banister and turned to look at her. "Have you looked around you, Erin? Have you seen the beauty of this place?"

"I have," she answered. "I wonder if you have."

"And what's that snide remark supposed to mean?" Devlin inquired with a lift of an eyebrow.

"I thought you were too busy looking at the daughter to notice the scenery."

Devlin chuckled. "I assumed that Myra was part of the scenery. She really didn't make that great an impression on me."

"I could tell," Erin sniped.

"Jealous?" Devlin quipped.

"Hardly," she came back, injecting a healthy disinterest in her denial. "I found it comical watching a middle-aged man making a fool of himself over a girl young enough to be his daughter."

"My daughter!" he bellowed. "My Lord, Erin. I'm not in my dotage yet. And Myra isn't young enough to be my daughter!" He stalked across the porch and poured himself a third cup of coffee. "I've known Wanda and Len for years," he commented.

"I'm not talking about her parents," Erin refuted, "or your friendship with them."

"Good morning! Good morning!" Raymond cried, rubbing his hands together, joining Devlin and Erin on the porch, stopping further barbs between them. "And what are we having for breakfast this morning?"

"Whatever you cook," Erin replied dryly. "I made the coffee, but I'm not cooking the breakfast."

Raymond picked up the empty saucer. "Looks like somebody had something to eat."

"Devlin made himself some toast."

"Toast!" Raymond sneered. "I need more nourishment than that. I'm a growing man."

"Oh, Raymond," Erin expostulated disgustedly, "all you think of is food. Every time I see you, you're stuffing your mouth."

"Come off it," Raymond snapped. "You've been on your high horse ever since we left San Antonio, and in particular you've been on my case. Now, hop off! I'm tired of it."

"Sorry," Erin sighed, instantly repentant. "I didn't

mean it." She shrugged. "I just don't know what's wrong with me."

"Well, I do," Raymond snorted, pouring himself a cup of coffee. "You're still angry because you had to ride down here with the Websters. And you're upset because Devlin and I rode down here with Alma and Myra." He chuckled softly. "You always like to make the arrangements, and this time someone took them out of your hands."

"Is the man telling the truth?" Devlin quizzed.

"Hardly," Erin returned calmly. "I'm just not accustomed to being away from the office like this. I'm missing an important meeting with Randolph Colton this morning, and I'm not sure that Ashley can handle it."

"You trained her, didn't you?" Raymond assured her.

"Quit worrying," Devlin advised her. "Have a good time. You'll be back there soon enough."

Erin stood to her feet, moving to the edge of the deck but standing away from Devlin. "I'm not worried," she said. "I'm bored." She flexed her shoulders, running her hands down her rib cage to her waist. I wish I hadn't let Raymond talk me into coming."

"But I'm glad that you did," Devlin said. "I think it's good for you. You needed to get away."

"And for the record," Raymond inserted, swinging his legs over the bench, huddling over the table, "I didn't talk you into coming. I simply pointed out the reasons why you should come." He lifted the cup to his lips, blowing. "If you're going to continue to renew these contracts we signed at the trade conference, you're gonna hafta mix with the people a little. Ya gotta be more sociable, Erin."

"Like me," Devlin boasted impishly, his eyes laughing at her.

"That'll be the day," Erin grated, walking down the steps into the lawn.

"You've got to climb out of that ivory tower you're

hiding in," Raymond philosophized between gulps of coffee.

"I'm not hiding in a tower," Erin vociferated heatedly, turning around to glare at both of them. "I'm tired of people accusing me of it." Her blue eyes, sparkling with anger, landed on Devlin.

He held his hands up innocently. "There must be some truth in what the man's saying," he argued, "for so many to have noticed."

"Being out here in the sticks isn't my idea of fun," Erin defended herself stoutly. "I don't care to sit around drinking, riding horses, boating, or telling stupid jokes."

"No one's doing that," Devlin returned, "and even if they were, it's not up to you to judge them. They've worked hard to have a successful conference, and now they want to relax and have a little fun. So what if they do act a little silly!"

He returned his cup to the tray. "Why can't you relax, Erin? Why can't you let your hair down?" Defensively Erin lifted her hand to her chignon even though she knew that he was speaking figuratively. "Designer skirt and shirt, I'll bet. Expensive sandals that match your outfit. Never a strand of hair out of place." His voice softened. "Why don't you learn to play a little, Erin?"

"Lecture me for judging," Erin countered. "Yet you dare point a finger and judge me." She took another step away from the deck. "I'm just bored, and I don't find the present company stimulating."

Devlin sprinted across the deck and down the steps, catching up with Erin. "Let me see if I can't be more stimulating." He picked her up and slung her over one shoulder. "A few kisses, a tumble on the grass," he grunted, carrying her across the lawn.

"Put me down!" Erin shouted, doubling her fists, pounding him on the back. "Somebody's going to see this!" She pelted him again, screaming, "Put me down right now. Do you hear me?"

He smacked her derriere soundly, then he jostled her to the ground like a sack of potatoes. "Can't help but hear you. You're shouting loud enough to wake the dead." Standing with his legs apart, his hands on his hips, he said, "This trip has been good for you. This is the first time I've seen you lose your cool. And you look pretty good when you're angry. And I know for sure that you're human."

"Too human, I'm afraid," she hissed irritably.

"Don't be ashamed of showing your emotions," he said quietly, falling in step with her, walking toward the river.

"Showing them is one thing," Erin asserted dryly. "Losing control of them is another."

About that time the sliding doors opened and Alma stepped onto the deck. "Raymond, we're cooking breakfast, and Myra is going to share some of her recipes with me. Come on in, and I'll let you choose your menu."

"Gorgeous," Raymond murmured, pushing the bench back, rising to his feet. "I knew you were an angel from the first moment that I laid eyes on you, Alma Cortez."

"Here," Alma beamed, "try this breakfast taco to tide you over until breakfast's done."

Swallowing the first bite, Raymond breathed, "Divine! Just what I needed."

Looking at Devlin and shaking her head in amused delight, Erin continued to walk toward the river. She was in no mood for their sweet talk, nor was she in the mood for Devlin this morning. He had angered her yesterday when he didn't insist on her riding with him and Raymond and when he lavished all his attention on Myra last evening.

"Care to go horseback riding," Devlin asked.

"No, I don't think so," she replied absently, lifting her hand to untangle her hair that had caught on a low-hanging branch.

"Why?"

"That's one sport I'm not very good at, and I'm afraid of horses. Also," she continued, "I really don't have the time to go riding. I'm going to be leaving this afternoon."

"Driving?"

"No, Raymond wants to stay, so he's going to drive me to the airport."

"You wouldn't consider staying one more night?"

"No."

"Are you really that bored?" he asked contemplatively. "I would think that this gorgeous countryside alone would be enough to keep anyone happy."

Erin shook her head. "No, I'm not bored, and I love this." She turned her face, her blue eyes clear and gentle. "This has been one of the most wonderful weekends in my entire life. The trade fair. Market Square."

"The Governor's Palace."

"Governor's Palace. Here."

"Don't go tonight," Devlin pleaded with urgency.

"I've got to. I can't miss the board meeting tomorrow."

"Call your father and have him reschedule it."

"I can't."

"My God!" he exclaimed. "Can't you forget business for one day? Can't you take an extra Monday and Tuesday off without feeling guilty? How long has it been since you've taken a vacation? How long since you've really left that damned office? Hmmm?"

"I'm quite selfish when it comes to considering my welfare," Erin defended herself softly. "And I'm also aware of my obligations to my job. I take my vacation when I feel that I need one, and I'll leave my office when I want." She thought for a second, then said, "I've just returned from Europe several weeks ago. That could be classified as getting away."

"Hardly," he scoffed. "You spent a week at the European trade fair. All work and no play!"

Erin could hardly stand the sarcastic accusation. "Is it wrong," she spat, "to be dedicated to your career? Is it wrong for me to enjoy working?"

"No," he grated, "it's not wrong to enjoy your job, but it's wrong to make a god and religion out of it."

"I don't do that," she shouted. "I enjoy it, and you're jealous because I happen to be good at it. You're upset because I'm throwing a kink in your merger plans. Well, Joe G. and the board can dictate a merger to take place between your company and mine, but they can't write me into the deal. And without me, Devlin Douglas, what kind of deal are you getting?"

"I'll get that merger on my terms," he promised her. "And I'll get you."

"I'm not a commodity to be bought or sold," she replied sharply. "And you'll never buy me. You'll get Lindsay Machinery if you want it badly enough, but you won't get me."

"You're speaking mighty boldly. I happen to know that you're in no bargaining position."

"Not boldly," Erin shot back, "truthfully. You won't get me unless I want you to have me. And that's the gospel, mister! As far as my bargaining position, I think it's time for you and me to sit down to discuss the terms of our merger." Since the time that topic had first come up, Erin's position had changed. It was now possibly to her advantage to agree to a merger. Provided that the terms Devlin offered suited her needs.

"I think it is too," he breathed, his eyes slit. "Shall we get a drink and discuss this in private?"

"We'll discuss it in your office as scheduled on Thursday morning."

Devlin crossed his arms over his chest, and he rocked back on his heels, steadily surveying Erin with interest. "Evidently your two days in market, little piggy, were good."

"Very good." She smirked her triumph.

"Are you sure that you don't want to discuss it with me now?" he asked.

Erin grinned. "I'm on holiday, Mr. Douglas. Away from the office. I wouldn't dare think about business today. It can wait until I get back."

Devlin chuckled. "The more I'm around you, Erin, the more I like you, and the more I respect you." He lifted a hand and rubbed his index finger alongside his nose. "But the more I dislike having you for a competitor."

"But it makes life more exciting, doesn't it?"

He shook his head. "I'm not sure that I like this kind of excitement. And I have a feeling that you've pulled a quick one on me."

"You'll find out Thursday, won't you?" she grinned.

"Sure you don't want to talk about it today?" he asked. When she shook her head, he suddenly laughed, exclaiming, "Okay! We'll play then! How about a quick boat ride?"

"Why not!" Erin acquiesced.

"Good! That's settled."

Erin stared at the cool, crystal water and murmured, "The river of no return." Aloud she warned, "If this is a guise to get me to discuss the merger, you're wasting your time."

"Word of honor," he drawled, raising his left hand. "I'm not going to give it another thought. I just want to show you the beautiful hill country, and we'll go for a hike. Okay?"

She nodded. "I just want to be sure that this attention is for me and not the merger."

"All of this is for you, little one," he promised. "As far as the merger is concerned, I can handle whatever comes. It may not be to my liking, but I'll take it at the right time. I never worry in advance about what may or could happen." He moved close to her, lifting his hand, gently trailing his fingers down the softness of her cheek. "I'm interested in Lindsay Machinery. Very interested. But at the moment I'm more interested in Erin Lindsay the woman."

Devlin's confession touched Erin's heart, thrilling her soul. "I almost believe you," she whispered. "And I'm almost frightened."

"I want you to believe me," he soughed, "but I don't want you frightened." His other hand came up, and he cupped her face. "I want to love you, Erin, if you'll give me the chance."

"No," she averred softly, "I can't give you the chance." Shaking her head, she added, "I will let you be my friend though."

"I can't accept only friendship," he sighed regretfully. "I want more than a platonic relationship. I want love. I want to make love to you."

"Devlin," Erin pleaded, "I don't think you've understood a word I've been telling you. I'm not part of a package deal. You're not going to get Lindsay Machinery because you get me or vice versa."

"I've never thought of you as part of the merger deal," he stated in ominous tones. "I've thought of you only as a woman. A woman that I want in my bed."

"And I've already informed you that you're not welcome in my bed," she reiterated.

"I'm not talking about your bed then," he countered smoothly. "I'm speaking about my bed. You're welcome there." The ebony eyes twinkled, and his lips curved upward in a teasing smile.

"You're shameless," Erin chuckled.

"No," he murmured, "just sure of what I want."

"I think I'll be safer riding that boat down the river than I will be in your bed."

Her laughter was a rich music that smothered Devlin with its sensual overtones. "You won't be safe either way," he replied, "if you're running from love."

"Could Raymond and Alma go with us?" she asked lightly, striving to hide her sudden shiver of apprehension.

Devlin's amusement erupted into deep, mellow laughter. "Safety in numbers?"

"Safety first," she quipped. "That's my motto."

"Are you afraid I'll take advantage of you?"

"Not really," she replied, placing her hands over his, pressing his warmth into her cheeks. "I think I'm afraid of your strength." The blue eyes were candid and honest. "I'm afraid of your determination."

He nodded. "I'm not a gentleman lover, if that's what you want, Erin. But I am a gentle lover. I'm a man who's worked his way up from the bottom. None of these fine finishing schools for me. No training in the social niceties or etiquette. Just like rumor has it, I'm crude and rough, yanked up by the bootstraps, and I did the yanking." He stepped even closer, his body almost touching hers, his breath warmly brushing the tendrils of curls around her face. "I'm not like those other milksops you've settled for for so long, and I'm not content to be a business associate held at arm's length, like Raymond."

"A warning?" she asked, her breathing slightly uneven, her heartbeat fast and hard.

"No," he denied, his eyes boldly sweeping over her face, over her body, making her tingle to life, making the blood pummel through her veins, making her aware of him as a man, of herself as a woman.

"A promise?"

When he nodded she forgot that he was her arch-rival; she forgot that he was the symbol of Douglas Enterprises, the symbol of what she had feared most in her career. At the moment he was a man who aroused every ounce of her femininity. Now Erin laughed, the sound exultant and rich. No man had ever excited her like Devlin did.

But there was no laughter reflected in the depths of those raven-colored eyes. Rather they mirrored a contemplative seriousness. His face lowered, his lips almost brushed hers. "What if I asked you for a kiss right now?" he said hoarsely.

"I'd say no," she returned quietly, never moving.

"I wonder," he mused on a soft note, dropping his hands, stepping back. "But I'll wait. There's no hurry, is there?" He reached out and caught her hand in his. "It's time we got moving if we're going boating and hiking in time for you to fly back to Houston."

She nodded, almost disappointed because he hadn't tried to kiss her.

"I'll go get the boat, and you can round up Raymond and Alma." He chuckled. "Reckon they can get away from the kitchen long enough to come."

Erin laughed with him. "Oh, yes, Raymond can get away from the kitchen, but he won't get away from the food. If I know him, he'll pack a picnic lunch to bring with him."

"Good idea," Devlin chortled. "I always knew Raymond was a good man, one with a head on his shoulders. Just tell him to pack a lunch big enough for all of us. I have a feeling that I'm going to need more for lunch than I had for breakfast."

He dropped her hand, going in one direction, leaving her to walk toward the house. After he had taken several steps, he stopped and turned.

"You're not going to change your mind, are you?"

"No," she replied, looking over her shoulder, "not unless you're going to try the Romeo bit."

"Are you interested in being Juliet?" he parried.

"No."

"Liar," he accused faintly. "I'll accept your answer for now. However, that doesn't mean that I won't keep trying to cast you in that role."

"I doubt you'll succeed."

"I don't often fail," he countered confidently.

"Then it's high time somebody brought you to the ground," Erin asserted. "It's time you learned humility."

Erin's riposte brought a soft chuckle from Devlin. "Not satisfied with my having lost the Cortez-Hernandez contract, not satisfied with your associate having won Alma Cortez's heart, and not satisfied with your having come between Myra and me," he teased, "you're wanting a pound of flesh as well. Shall I call you Shylock?"

"If I don't want to be cast as Juliet," Erin quipped, "then I certainly don't want to be compared to Shylock."

"No," he whispered, his eyes slowly memorizing each feature of her face, "I don't think you look like a Shylock either."

The hot touch of his eyes almost rendered Erin speechless. Eventually she said, "Then don't call me Shylock."

"How about darling, sweetheart, precious, or . . ."

She shook her head, melting from the heated intimacy of his smile and his words. His promise nearly suffocated her with its amorous desire.

Devlin saw the desire as it lapped into flame in Erin's eyes, and he felt her reciprocation. "Don't invite Raymond or Alma," he softly enjoined her. "Let's go by ourselves."

Erin smiled tenderly and shook her head. "Don't ask this of me yet, Devlin. I'm going to play awhile, but you'll have to let me set the rules of the game."

"Okay," he sighed patiently, disappointment echoed in the ebony eyes. "You can choose the rules . . . for a while longer."

CHAPTER FOUR

Devlin stood in front of his desk, his gaze fixed on Erin, who walked through the door. Red must be her favorite color, he thought, taking notice of her red long-sleeved blouse with the huge, floppy bow that contrasted with her black, V-necked, two-button blazer and straight skirt. And, he decided at that same moment, it was a color that looked good on her, complimenting her fair complexion and her blond hair. As his eyes swept over the sedate bun, he suppressed a grin. For Erin the trade fair was over, the holidays gone.

"I'm glad you came." He welcomed her with a large smile of pleasure. "I wondered if you would."

"I wouldn't have missed this for anything," she returned easily, looking around the office, liking the bold greens and blues that were held together by the soft ecru.

The thick, soft carpet, the round conference desk in the corner, the rich, elegant chairs in front of his desk, the elaborate bar set off in one corner, all reflected the sheer opulence of his office. Yet simplicity dominated there, and neither the colors nor the furniture overshadowed the powerful man who stood in front of his desk, arms crossed over his chest.

"The trade fair seems to have been good for you," Devlin commented, walking to the large window that extended across the width of one wall.

"It was," Erin agreed, enjoying the brilliant burst of sunlight that gushed into the room when Devlin pulled the drape.

"And the holidays," he asked softly, "were they good for you too?"

Erin shrugged, dropping her red shoulder purse and her portfolio onto the table beside the chair nearest her. "They weren't bad."

"But not good either," Devlin parried, a small frown line creasing his forehead, his eyes narrowing.

The blue eyes that directly encountered the black ones were cool. "As far as holidays go," Erin announced in stilted tones, sitting down, "they were wonderful. But," she smiled, "holidays are over, and it's time to work."

Devlin settled his large frame on the edge of his desk, and he gently swung one of his legs, balancing his weight with the other one. "I should have known," he thrummed softly.

"You should have," Erin retorted distantly but assuredly. "It was my understanding that we meet today to discuss the merger. I believe you were going to point out the advantages of doing business the Douglas way."

"Was I?" he murmured, his eyes slowly, familiarly, exploring every inch of her tall, lissome body.

"You were," Erin returned steadily, not allowing him to beguile her with either sweet talk or sweet actions.

Deliberately she avoided prolonged eye contact. She had learned during the past few days that Devlin Douglas was a devastating man, one of great purpose and determination. Also she had learned that he was in no hurry to get what he wanted, and he wanted Lindsay Machinery and her with it.

"And it was my understanding, Ms. Lindsay, that you have something of interest to tell me."

"I have something to tell you," she concurred, lifting her face, looking straight into those dark eyes, "but whether it's of interest to you, you'll have to judge."

She wanted to withdraw her gaze, but Devlin held it, his eyes transmitting sensual waves that acted like magnets, pulling Erin to him, binding her to him. "Anything you say or do is of interest to me," he informed her, those ebony eyes, blazing with passion, desperately trying to transmit their burning message to Erin. "But I haven't proved that to you yet, have I?" he asked sadly, watching her movements, liking what he saw, liking what he felt. "You still don't believe me."

Feeling that inexplicable bonding and resenting it, Erin stood and walked to the window, turning her back to Devlin. She had to break the shroud of intimacy that Devlin was attempting to wrap around her, and she had to quell those responding tendencies of hers that were more dangerous than his advances.

At length Erin spoke. "I believe you," she averred softly, the low sound sultry and husky. "But I'm not interested."

She turned slowly, letting her eyes randomly wander around the room, seeing a pair of black-rimmed glasses on an open file on the desk. Searching for some way to break the tense silence of the moment, she turned to desultory conversation.

"I don't remember your wearing glasses."

"Anything to change the conversation, Erin." He chuckled in spite of himself and dropped his head. "I do wear glasses when I read. You've probably never noticed because you haven't been around me that much." He walked to the desk, picked them up, and slid them into their leather case. "You don't wear glasses?"

"No," Erin retorted spiritedly, her eyes warm and sparkling, her lips spiced with a smile of unadulterated mirth. "You're forgetting," she quietly pointed out, "you're much older than I am."

"Old enough but not too old," he shot back, his eyes never wavering from her face, defying her to look away. "Old enough to know what I want from life and young enough to take it."

For endless seconds they stared at each other, oblivious to time or place, bound together in communicative silence. When the intercom buzzed, Devlin, with hardly any movement of his fingers, pressed the button and lifted the receiver, never taking his eyes from Erin's face. "Douglas." Slowly he smiled over the phone at Erin, and her lips, tremulous and soft, responded. "Thanks, Debbie. Send them in. We're ready." As he replaced the receiver on the cradle, he spoke to Erin, walking to the large round table in the far corner of the room. "Why don't you come over here? Sam and Wallace are coming in." He pulled one of the chairs from the table and motioned for her. "The three of us work closely together."

Erin sat down at about the time the door opened and the two men walked in. Quickly introductions were made, and business was begun. Quite ably Devlin shifted from the warm, gentle lover to an efficient and brisk executive, moving the conversation from sparring to casual quips to the merger. Succinctly he pointed out the advantages of such a consolidation between Lindsay Machinery and Douglas Enterprises, and he stressed the importance of Erin's remaining president of Lindsay Machinery. When he had concluded, he asked Sam Edgerton and Wallace Stevenson to outline the specific terms of their proposal.

Erin listened quietly, assimilating all they said, looking carefully at the data sheets they periodically handed her, studying them, making meticulous notes. But not once did she let them or Devlin read more on her face than she wanted them to. Not once did she lower her guard. As easily, as efficiently, and as quickly as Devlin, she dropped the cloak of friendship to become Erin Lindsay, president of Lindsay Machinery.

Although Erin concurred with most of the facts that the committee had so diligently and punctiliously researched and that Devlin had so painstakingly pointed out, she didn't commit herself one way or the other. She had done some research of her own on Devlin's firm and after she listened, she refuted and questioned. But she made no impulsive or rash promises. She did, however, promise to present his offer to her board of directors for their advice and consideration.

"As you gentlemen know," Erin said, "until recently our directors have felt that we had no alternative but a merger with Douglas Enterprises. At our last meeting, however, I was able to point out another one. This new alternative is the reason why only I came for this briefing today. I'll report back to the directors, but I don't pretend to know what their answer will be."

Now Devlin understood why Erin had insisted on returning to Houston for that board meeting. He took off his glasses and laid them on the table, pushing back in his chair. "Your alternative can't be as advantageous to your company as a merger with us," he summed up. "As you can see—" he paused, looking directly into those shining blue eyes that were as beautiful as they were cool and untouchable "—a merger would benefit both of us."

"And from the way you've outlined it," Erin asserted, a soundless chuckle escaping the full, red lips, "more beneficial to Douglas Enterprises than to Lindsay Machinery."

Sam's wrinkled face creased into a patronizing smile. He'd teach Joe Lindsay to send a woman to do a man's job. "When you're holding the short end of the stick, Ms. Lindsay, what can you expect?"

"I heard exactly what I expected, Mr. Edgerton," Erin returned smoothly. "But I must refute your last statement. Lindsay Machinery is not on the short end of the stick, as you so inaptly described."

Sam winked at Devlin and Wallace, and the three of them chuckled quietly. "We admire and respect your judgment, but we're not going to let you bluff us by your cool appearance and tough words. Nor are we going to let you blind our better judgment with your beauty."

"Mr. Edgerton," Erin rejoined coolly, snapping the top of her pen, dropping it and her notebook into her portfolio, "I do not appreciate your acting in such an unbusinesslike manner." She pulled out three packets of data sheets that she had compiled, and, still standing, she handed one to each man. "Please read these at your leisure, gentlemen. I'm sure that once you've acquainted yourself with these facts and figures, you'll reevaluate your present demands." She looked at Wallace, then Sam. "Thanks to both of you for a very enlightening report. I assure you that I will present all you have said and all you have not said to my board of directors." She walked to the window and stared at the busy freeway traffic that bustled to and fro. "And, gentlemen, until you come up with more equitable terms, there is no way I would consent to remain with Lindsay Machinery if a merger should come to pass."

"What are your terms for remaining?" Devlin asked, moving closer to the desk, picking up the folder of papers and flipping through the pages slowly.

She turned, facing the conference table. "I've outlined a counterproposal which I've submitted in writing. After the three of you have read and studied it, possibly discussed it, why don't you contact me. I've been authorized by the board to work out a merger plan that is feasible for both of us, one that is not so one-sided."

A little more subdued than he had been in the beginning, Sam looked up from his copy of Erin's proposal. "You weren't bluffing."

"No, Mr. Edgerton," Erin retorted, crossing her legs at the ankles and leaning against the window casement. "I wasn't bluffing."

Devlin shuffled his papers together and slid his glasses into his case. "As I said before, Erin, the trade fair was very good for you."

Erin smiled, truly the victor.

Following Devlin's lead, the two men gathered their papers together and as unobtrusively as the introductions had been made, the good-byes were said, with Sam and Wallace filing out of the room, leaving Erin and Devlin alone once more. Erin walked to the table and picked up her portfolio, carrying it to the chair where her purse lay. As her hand folded around her purse, she heard Devlin's voice.

"Don't rush off!" The deep, resonant tones compelled Erin to sit down while the ebony eyes soothed away her irritation at his having issued the command.

Again their verbal dueling resumed, each testing the other, baiting, biting, retreating, advancing again. First one tactic, then another, with Devlin totally captivating Erin. The merger was the farthest thing from his mind, the nearest for her.

"How about a cup of coffee?" he asked.

"Half a cup, please."

"Just enough cream to color and no sugar," he murmured.

"You remembered," she marveled, twisting to take her jacket off. Then she felt his fingers as they brushed against her shoulders when he helped her. The touch was deliberate; it was planned. She knew it, and the tender mockery that danced in his eyes affirmed her suspicion.

"I haven't forgotten anything about you," he stated

softly, walking to the ornate serving bar, pouring the coffee. "We have only the powdered cream," he told her. "Perhaps you'd like to measure it for yourself."

Erin stood, obeying his command as if it were an everyday occurrence. She walked across the plush carpet, her red and black high-heeled sandals sinking into the pile. Just as she reached the bar, just as she held her hand out for the spoon, however, something happened, and she tripped; she stumbled.

"Are you all right?" he asked, catching her, his hands clasping her shoulders, the heat of each finger burning through the flimsy crepe material.

"I think so," she muttered, her blue eyes puzzled. "I don't know what happened."

"You tripped," he explained, laughter bubbling in the dark recesses of those eyes. "This is getting to be a habit, isn't it?"

"It is," she whispered, looking into his face, making no attempt to push out of his arms, watching the wicked sparks as they flashed in the fathomless pits of ebony. "And this time," she accused, "it was your fault." He laughed his pleasure, but even this didn't jar her out of his arms. "I think you deliberately tripped me."

"But you don't know that for sure," he teased her.

"No, I'll never know for sure," she agreed, not budging, hardly daring to breathe. Only the increased rhythm of her heart and the little-girl wonder in her eyes betrayed the depth of her emotions.

The silence stretched between them, electric as their touch, as their seeing, as their longing for each other. He held her loosely in his arms, quietly and comfortably, safe and secure. At the same time they absorbed the vital force that flowed between them, making them one, filling each with a piercing awareness of what was going to happen when either of them moved.

"I think I shall have to kiss you. I hope you're not going

to protest." His voice, slightly husky, deep, and gravelly, rang seductively in her ears.

She shook her head. "No—" She began, licking her lips. "I mean—" She faltered, desperately trying to marshal her thoughts. "I'm not—"

Devlin's head came nearer, and his lips hovered above hers, their breath mingling together, the soft warmth becoming a vapor of suspended ecstasy. "What will you do, I wonder."

She didn't answer. In truth, she couldn't answer. Her lips began to tremble with desire; they began to pout for his kiss. Then his lips touched hers in sweet, quick nibbles.

"I think, Erin, I shall have to take my chances. The temptation is much too strong to resist."

His mouth closed over hers, warmly gentle, begging for her response, delighting when she began to explore with him. They discovered the feel and texture of each other's lips. They tasted the delicious flavor of each other's mouth, his tongue and hers meeting in tentative greeting first, sending excruciating delight shivering through Erin's limbs. Devlin sighed softly and lifted his lips, feathering them softly over her flushed cheeks, into her temples, around her ears. Finding that pleasure point at the base of her ear, he nuzzled softly, driving Erin wild with his strokes.

Then his lips claimed hers again, and his hands glided down the length of her back, over the soft curves of her bottom, cupping her, lifting her against the hardness of his body. Erin faintly moaned her acquiescence, her arms closing about his shoulders, her hands tenaciously clutching him, her fingers biting into his flesh.

Both were caught up in a purely physical reaction that neither could explain. It wasn't as if Erin were an inexperienced teenager; it wasn't as if Devlin were an overaged adolescent. There was no reason for their fevered desires. No reason why their passion should transcend coherent thought. Yet as their hands moved randomly, acquainting each other with the touch and feel, as their lips sampled the delights of their body and skin, they sensed the hunger in each other. They could feel their aroused passion.

They pulled apart, their breathing ragged, and they stood for a long time, staring at each other. Devlin's hands came up to her hair, touching the mussed curls. "Do you always wear your hair up like this or tied back on your neck?"

She nodded her head, running her tongue over her swollen, throbbing lips. "Most of the time."

"Do you ever let it hang freely around your face?" he asked softly, pulling away just enough to peer at her.

"At night," she whispered. "When I'm going to bed."

"Ahhh," he droned seductively, his fingers deftly reaching for the hairpins, dropping them carelessly on the floor. As her hair fell around her face, golden waves cascading around her shoulders in wild abandon, flames of erotic desire leaped in Devlin's ebony eyes. "You look like an angel." His hands cupped her shoulders, and he stared into her face. "Erin—" He paused, his eyes touching each feature of her face. "Erin." Thoughtfully he repeated her name, letting it slowly fade into quietness.

He wasn't tongue-tied. He was just stupefied. He couldn't understand himself or his actions. Usually the first time he kissed a woman it was purely experimental, a curiosity more than a caress. But this had gotten out of hand, and he could still feel the fire burning in his groin. And it had confirmed his suspicions. He wanted more than kisses; he wanted more than just sex.

He shook his head. "I knew—but I didn't realize just how much—I'm—" He was speechless. No words could express the tenderness and the longing that he felt for Erin.

Thinking he was about to apologize, Erin moved away from him, hugging her arms tightly around herself. Her fingers gripped the soft flesh of her upper arms that were covered by the thin layer of red crepe. She smiled stiffly.

"Don't apologize," she whispered with a defiant swing of her head. "I wanted you to kiss me. . . . I'm glad that you did."

Devlin shook his head, a strange smile playing around his mouth. "No," he drawled slowly, "you've got it all wrong. I'm not apologizing, not even thinking about it. I'm figuring out a way to ask you to spend the night with me without your thinking the worst of me."

"Part of your tactics to get the company?"

"That's what I was afraid you'd think." He grimaced, disappointed, walking to the bar to pour himself another cup of coffee. "No," he breathed wearily, "it's not another tactic to get your company. It just happened. You knew it would eventually; so did I." He smiled, holding the coffeepot toward her. "Want to try the coffee again?"

A cup of coffee! she thought, dazed. A cup of coffee! *Who wants a cup of coffee after this?* She was angry because he didn't seem to be upset or disturbed by the kiss. He just wanted her in his bed.

"Well," he pressed. "Coffee or not?"

She shook her head, moving restlessly around the room. "No, thanks."

Devlin poured his coffee, returned the pot to the warmer, and lifted the cup to his lips, watching Erin as she walked around. He enjoyed the pull of the straight black skirt that cupped the firm, fully rounded hips, the stretch of the material that accented her slender, well-proportioned legs, the slit that revealed the satin skin of her lower thighs.

"Just because I kissed you," she began in a low, steady voice, "just because I enjoyed kissing you, doesn't mean that I'm ready to jump into bed with you."

"I know," he rejoined softly. "That's why I was taking my time. That's why I sounded like a stammering schoolboy. I knew that you would have a difficult time accepting it." He smiled tenderly. "Perhaps a cup of coffee would help."

"Would help what?" Erin snapped, edgy and defensive.

"Your nervousness," he pointed out. "You're about to wear a hole in my carpet where you've walked back and forth."

"I'm not nervous," she exploded.

"I know," he said, lifting the coffeepot once again, pouring another cup of coffee, and adding a spoon of powdered cream. "You're just like me." He carried the cup to her and pressed it into her hands. "You can't believe what we just experienced. But it's real, Erin, and I do care. Really care about you!"

"Can't you get it through your head, Devlin," she cried, moving to the bar, setting the cup down with a thud, "that I don't want you to care. I don't want you in my life."

"I wish that was *all* I wanted," he returned. "It would be so much simpler. But I want more, Erin. I must be in your heart."

"I don't care what you want," she added.

"Yes," he contradicted her softly, "you care. And it's hurting you like hell right now because you think my actions are motivated by my desire to have Lindsay Machinery. You're agonizing because part of you wants to believe what I'm saying, but the other part is too maimed and hurt to believe."

"You don't know what I'm thinking," Erin blared out, uneasy because he was reading her heart and treading on her feelings. "And you don't know what I'm feeling. You're just guessing, trying to push me into admitting that I want you."

She walked to the spot where Devlin had held her when he kissed her, to the spot where she had submissively allowed him to pull the pins from her hair. Stooping, she picked them up one by one.

"Well, don't congratulate yourself too soon," she spat out. "I'm not about to admit it. Unlike you, I don't go around pretending."

She straightened and walked to the large baroque mirror that hung over the conference table. Facing Devlin, her back to the mirror, she said, "My response to you was purely physical. Nothing more than curiosity. And even if it were more, I don't want you in my heart. I don't have room for you there."

"You may not want me in your heart yet," Devlin conceded, "but I know that you want me in your bed."

Angrily Erin spun around and twisted her hair into a knot, poking the pins in unceremoniously. "Think what you will," she gritted through clenched teeth.

"We may start with the bed," Devlin quietly asserted, the timbre of his voice lighting brushfires of desire that burned throughout her, "but I'll end up in your heart. You were right last Monday when you described the river as being one of no return. You made a decision that moment, and there's no turning back. From now on your life is bound to mine."

"No," she whispered, "that's not true."

"Yes," he softly countered, "it's true, and it's what you're fighting."

Through the mirror Erin watched Devlin set his cup down. She watched as he stared directly into the mirror, staring beyond her into her soul. She wanted to reach up with her hands to hide her vulnerability. She didn't want him to see beyond the cold exterior. That was her only protection.

"I'm going to melt that frozen iceberg that surrounds your heart, Erin, and I'll burn your resistance until it crumbles into ashes around your feet."

As he talked he moved closer and closer until he stood directly behind her, his hands clasping her shoulders, his touch searing through the silk to her flesh. She knew that with the touch he had claimed her soul and had branded it with his love.

"You're quite sure of yourself," she taunted in her honey-smooth voice, her face swinging around, her lips lightly brushing against the knuckles of his hands, which still rested on her shoulders.

"I don't have time for nonsense, so when I want something I go after it with the idea of getting it."

"No holds barred," Erin softly averred. "No thought for the other person."

"No holds barred!"

The maneuver was so quick, so well executed, she found herself looking directly into Devlin's face, confronting those eyes that burned so passionately, searing into her soul, destroying any inhibitions she might have had. Valiantly she struggled, and she won. Lowering her face, she twisted her shoulders and broke from his grasp.

Slowly she stepped back, moving out of his staked territory. She moved smoothly and steadily but not fast. She didn't want him to get the impression that she was retreating. It was a planned movement to give her the space she needed to think and to initiate her next move. She looked at the small diamond watch that adorned her left arm. Then she moved to the table where her things were.

"Going?" Devlin asked, walking to his desk, watching her slip into her jacket.

"Going."

"I had thought that we'd have lunch together. I've made reservations at—"

"No, thanks," she murmured, picking up her purse.

"Will I see you again?"

"Maybe." Her hand folded around the portfolio.

"When?"

"When we discuss the counterproposal."

"Why?" The ebony eyes narrowed.

"I never gave you reason to think differently," she returned, running a hand down the front of her jacket, smoothing out the creases. "I'm not sure that we ought to see each other again."

"Do you really expect me to believe that you're not going to see me before that?"

"I wonder about the wisdom of my seeing you again." She pulled the strap of her purse a little higher on her shoulder and shifted the portfolio from her hand to under her arm.

"You will, you know."

He moved away from the desk, and before Erin knew it he was standing in front of her, slipping her purse strap off her shoulder, taking her portfolio in his other hand, throwing it into the chair.

"Yes, I know it," she confirmed softly, "but you don't have to sound so cocky about it."

"I'm not," he confessed. "I just sound that way. Deep inside I'm trembling with apprehension." He smiled. "Will you have dinner with me tonight?"

She nodded, mesmerized by his head, which came closer and closer, excited by the feel of his hands that cupped her face. His thumbs, reminiscent of another day, rested on the corners of her mouth, and his fingers splayed across her cheeks.

"I can't let you go without doing this," he owned softly. His lips hovered above hers. So close yet so far away. "And if we weren't in my office, I would do more than this." His lips touched hers lightly and experimentally, as if he were tasting them for the first time, as if they were a new delicacy. He whispered a sigh just as his mouth, at once rough, again tender, took possession of hers in another and another of those deep kisses that dissolved all resistance, reducing her to a molten mass of utter femininity.

Erin didn't take the time to reason or to recriminate herself; she liked the feel of those powerful arms around her. She enjoyed the warmth of his body, and she felt secure and safe. She freely allowed her arms to slip around his body, to cradle the flexed muscles of his back. And when he pulled his lips from hers, murmuring incoherent words of love in her ears, she pressed closer to him, turning his face, her lips hungrily seeking his.

"Your body believes me," he breathed into her mouth. "Why can't your brain accept it?"

"Don't talk so much," she whispered. She nestled closer to him. "Just kiss me."

Devlin accepted this as a token of her surrender, and it was. Not that she planned it this way. It simply happened. He pulled her nearer, held her more tightly, his hands sending erotic messages to her body as they meandered lovingly up and down her spine, coming to rest on the swell of her buttocks, both hands cupping the voluptuous curves. Erin could feel the hotness of his fingers through the thin material of her skirt, their strength burning sweetly to her senses.

"You smell good," she murmured, burrowing her cheek against the soft fabric of his shirt. "Woodsy and clean."

Her words slithered across his heart, and he lowered his face at the same time she lifted hers, her lips tremulous for his kisses. Disobeying her own rule of never becoming involved with a man, Erin's lips and actions communicated just the opposite. And as Devlin kissed her, as the kiss deepened, he took complete possession of her mouth, a forewarning of the way he would take possession of her entire body, eventually reaching her heart and her soul.

His tongue, insistent and demanding, boldly entered that spicy cave, finding all the secret places of delight, exploring, mapping, whetting the want that he knew was somewhere beneath all the camouflage. He let her know in no uncertain terms that he wouldn't settle for less than all of her. He told her with his mouth, his tongue, his hands, the hardness of his muscular frame.

When he withdrew his lips, he teased the corners of her

mouth with slow, warm nibbles, his arms still cradling her close to him. She savored the warmth of his breath, the moistness of his soft, firm lips, the heat of his hands as they continued to cup and knead her buttocks.

"Oh, God, Erin!" he sighed heavily in her ear. "Be glad I don't have a bed in my office. I promise you I would be tempted, strongly tempted to do more than kiss you."

"Would you?" she murmured lovingly, joining in his fantasy, her voice faraway and dreamy. Her face nestled against the material of his suit, her fingers played with his tie, and she listened to the heavy and erratic music of his heart.

"I said that," he confessed slowly, breathing deeply, "but I don't think I could."

Erin tensed, and she tried to pull out of his arms. "I don't understand you," she whispered, hurt shafting through her slender frame.

His arms tightened around her, and he drew her back into the protective shelter of his body. "Making love to you for a night would be wonderful, I admit." Again he paused, his hands moving in exquisite smoothness up and down her back. "But I don't think I can be satisfied with less than all of you, Erin. Your body, your mind, your soul!" He breathed deeply, perplexed with himself, not understanding his obsession to possess Erin totally.

"That's sort of frightening," she replied, her head safely tucked on his chest, her breathing coinciding with the increased cadence of his heart.

"Why should it be?" he asked, his chin brushing the top of her golden hair.

"Men have possessed my body," she said quietly, not bothering to tell him that Ralph was the only man to have made love to her. "But no man," she avowed, pushing herself away from the protective haven of his closeness, "has ever possessed my soul. No man has been privileged to see it, much less have it."

Devlin smiled, not perturbed by her words, not concerned with what had been, concerned only with what would be. The past he couldn't redo, so he left it behind; he concentrated on the future.

"If no man has possessed your soul, my darling, then no man has possessed you. He may have had sex with you, but he didn't possess you. He didn't make love to you." His eyes flamed with desire, transplanting a part of his deep-seated want in the core of her being. "I'll make another promise to you." The words were intimate and silky. "You will possess me in the same way, and you won't be satisfied with just loving my body. You'll want to love more of me." His hands moved to her face again, framing it, holding it with tenderness. "And I'll set your mind at ease. I won't possess your body until I know that you're giving me all of you."

A haunting sadness filled her eyes before it overflowed and spread throughout her body. "That's what I was afraid of," she admitted. "And now I'll promise you something. You will probably never possess me in the sense that you're talking about. And if—" she hesitated "—if you should, you may have to wait a long, long time."

"I may wait a long time," he agreed, "but I will have you, all of you."

"I've never given a man that privilege," she asserted. "But you may try. I'm sure that both of us will enjoy the pursuit."

Something flickered in those raven-black eyes, a certain momentary satisfaction. He was going to thoroughly enjoy this woman. She knew how to battle, she enjoyed battle, and she wasn't afraid of him.

His blood ran hot through his body, and he felt his surging desire. He could hardly wait for tonight. "Too late, Erin," he warned, "I'm almost already there. The hunt began the moment you walked into that dining room at the Quail Ridge Dairy Farm. You're almost mine now."

"Really?" Erin quipped, recognizing the truth of his declaration, understanding why he thought this. Certainly she had responded to him today, but she wouldn't give him the satisfaction of knowing for sure. Nor would she let him know just how deeply he had affected her.

Stepping back, not replying, Devlin's raven eyes slowly winged over her body, making her aware of all the places he had caressed her body. He eventually said, "All your denials won't change the truth, Erin."

Looking at his dark masculinity, understanding him, Erin knew that he wanted no less than her soul. He wanted her most precious possession—that one gift she had shared with no man. And, she realized, if she weren't extremely careful, always a step ahead of him, he wouldn't have to take her heart from her. She would hand it to him.

"It doesn't pay to be overconfident." She lifted her arm, giving a hasty glance at her watch. "I have to run now."

"I'm not overconfident," he told her again. He smiled. "If you've responded like this the first time I really kissed you, what will happen tonight when we're alone?"

"I'd better see to it, then, that we're not alone," she murmured, desire butterflying through her stomach.

"Even if you succeed in seeing that we're not alone tonight, what about tomorrow night, or the night after that?"

"I see that you've got a one-track mind," she teased. "Maybe I'd better plan for our dinner tonight."

"Whatever pleases you," he conceded easily, not minding. "But when the time comes, I guarantee you that I'll find us a secluded spot, a spot all our own."

CHAPTER FIVE

Erin gazed at herself with satisfaction, enjoying the transformation from career woman to romantic lady. She smiled, her lips a soft, delicate pink, innocently provocative, her cheeks blushing with the same gentle color. Her blue eyes, glowing with excitement, were enhanced and intensified by mascara and eye shadow. Her blond hair, as usual, was coiffed in an elegant upsweep of curls, but tonight she intentionally broke the customary severity by letting some strands enticingly wisp around her neck and face. The chignon of loose curls was secured and decorated with tiny threads of silk and gold, interwoven with pearls.

She turned around, pirouetting in front of the full-length mirror, admiring her newest purchase. She had been saving it for another time, but she admitted with a satisfied smile that tonight seemed to be the perfect occasion after all. The blue-green evening gown that covered her body from neck to toe hung in flowing lines from the waist, the silk accenting her gentle curves. The lace mandarin collar hid the graceful length of her neck, but it brought full attention to the shoulders and the upper swell of her breasts, which were caressed with the delicate Brussels lace in the same color as the gown. A pearl, ensconced in a circlet of diamonds, decorated the lobe of each ear.

Clutching her evening bag in her hand, she walked out of the bedroom, turning the light off as she stepped into the living room, glancing at the huge grandfather clock that stood majestically in the corner of the commodious room. Though the furniture was large, it wasn't bulky, nor did it crowd the room. Rather, it complemented the spaciousness, its colors and style tropical rattan, a total extension of Erin. It wasn't difficult to gather that she was an earthy woman who enjoyed the primitive sensuality of nature, basking in its vibrant, hot colors.

The chair, the love seat, and the divan, placed in a large horseshoe, were upholstered in a rich, warm brown floral print. The exotic flowers that covered the brown background were bright oranges, tans, and beiges. Two large square end tables, glass and rattan, adorned one end of the sofa and one side of the occasional chair, and the love seat formed the bottom of the U-shaped grouping. All these pieces curved around a large rattan and glass coffee table that dominated the center of the room, resting elegantly on the thick plushness of the terra-cotta carpet.

On her way to draw the drapes, Erin switched on the two table lamps, letting the soft light filter through the room, creating a feeling of comfort but not a seductive scene. Though she knew that she would eventually go to bed with Devlin, she was biding her time. Her face, softened by her happiness, gently swept around the room, glancing at the bar, which was tastefully simple, another extension of the decor. Everything was ready, she concluded, pleased with her preparations, moving to the stereo that lined one wall, flicking the knob, letting the soft music flow into the room. At the same time she heard the faint sound of her door chimes.

Walking through the living room into the foyer, Erin's

smile became more than a gesture of the lips; it radiated her inner self. However, when she opened the door, she was momentarily disconcerted. Devlin wasn't dressed formally. Instead, he still wore the gray slacks and the vest that he'd worn at his office earlier, but now the collar was unbuttoned and his tie hung loosely around his neck.

"Hi," he murmured, running his dark eyes over her in admiration. "You look beautiful." As he spoke he glanced over her shoulder to the warmth and comfort of the room.

Stepping back, she motioned him into the house. "Want to come in for a drink?"

He smiled, and she could see the lines of weariness around his eyes and the deep grooves at the corners of his mouth. "I'd like that," he replied tiredly, using his shoulder to lever away from the red brick wall.

"You look exhausted," she observed, leading the way into the living room.

"I am." He almost groaned, sinking into the cushiony softness of the sofa, lying his head against the pillowed back. "I've been running ever since you left." He sighed. "This feels good. I could just lie here and not move for a month."

"Won't be long until the Thanksgiving holidays," Erin supplied, understanding his exhaustion.

He nodded slowly, closing his eyes. "Think I can make it till next Thursday?"

"I think so," she murmured, walking to the bar. "What do you prefer?"

"Scotch and water, if you have it."

She nodded, busying herself with the task of preparing the drinks, her sounds pleasing Devlin. The soft humming. The gentle swish of her gown as she moved. The tinkle of ice as it dropped into the glass. The splash of the liquor. All of it produced an altogether homey and inviting scene.

"Has it been one of those days?" Erin asked when she noticed his furrowed brow.

"Uh-huh," he droned, shaking off his loneliness, feeling her approach more than hearing it. Slowly he forced his heavy lashes up, encountering the glass with its amber-colored liquor and the cubes of glittering ice. He lifted his hand, grasping the drink, cupping it in both hands. "Thanks."

Levering himself up, he sat, flexing his shoulders as if he could dispel the exhaustion that had finally caught up with him. After taking several swallows of his drink, he rolled the glass between the palms of his hands and lowered his head, looking at the liquor. Suddenly he felt his tiredness, not just the tiredness of the day, but the tiredness of the past few years since Nancy had died. He felt that acute loneliness that he'd felt earlier today when Erin had left the office.

He lifted his head and stared across the room. "Are you ready?" he asked.

"I am," she rejoined softly. "The question is, are you?"

He smiled apologetically, looking down at his business suit. "Sorry. Last-minute negotiations. Since I didn't want to keep you waiting, I didn't take the time to change."

"Would you like to have dinner here?" Erin found herself saying.

"Do you know what you're asking?" His ebony eyes pierced hers.

"I know."

"And you're ready for it?"

"I think so."

Her tentative reply was his answer. "I think we'd better go out."

"I'd like to prepare dinner for you."

"I want you to be sure, Erin. Very sure."

"I'm sure about dinner," she returned, a glimmer of laughter in the blue eyes.

His snort of laughter was low. "I think dinner is the least of my concerns at the moment. And our eating here wouldn't be fair to you." His eyes swept over her evening gown. "It's hardly a night out for you."

"I don't mind. A night in sounds good to me, and it's what the doctor ordered for you." Now it was her turn to smile and to surprise him. "I'm really not an awful cook, if that's what's bothering you." She chuckled, walking toward the kitchen. "In fact, I'm quite domesticated. Contrary to rumor, I do my own cooking, cleaning, and washing."

"No gold spoon in your mouth?" he asked, leaning back on the couch.

"Not a gold one," she retorted. "A silver one, but certainly not a gold one." She walked across the terra-cotta carpet, stepping through the arch into the dining room. She stopped in the archway, one hand on the collar of her gown, the other resting lightly on the wall. "My mother, however, always said that if you were lucky enough to have been born with a silver spoon in your mouth, you should have enough wisdom and intelligence to keep it polished and shining." She smiled, her eyes bright with pleasant memories. "She spent her short life teaching me how to take care of it."

"Are you going to cook in that get-up?" he asked curiously.

She laughed. "Just might. Right now, though, I'm going to scour the pantry to see what I can cook on such short notice." She took another step. "You make yourself comfortable, and I'll be right back." She pointed to the bookshelves that lined one of the walls. "You can watch television if you want to. Open the top doors."

Devlin nodded, stood, and moved in the direction she indicated. "I think I will." He set his glass on the coffee table and shucked his vest and tie, rolling his shirt sleeves up a cuff or two. After he turned on the television, he slipped his shoes off and lay back on the sofa.

Erin, in the meantime, had thoroughly searched the larder. "Cold cuts or steak?" she asked, pushing through the swinging doors that separated the dining room from the kitchen. "If it's sandwiches, I can have dinner in record time. If it's steak, it'll take longer."

"Which do you prefer?" he parried, wanting more than cold cuts but willing to accept whatever she offered to prepare.

"Your choice," she deferred.

Devlin, still lying on the sofa, his eyes glued to her, held his hand out, and Erin, obeying the silent summons, crossed the floor. She stood at his side, looking down at him, placing her hand in his. Almost as if she were transfixed, she stared at the strong but gentle hand that clasped hers. She liked the latent strength she could feel; she liked the warmth and security it provided.

"I'm hungry," he told her. "Terribly hungry. I haven't taken the time to eat all day, and I'm bushed." She could see the tiredness in his eyes; she could hear it in his voice. "The steak sounds great. Would you?"

"Surely," she said softly, her reply womanly sweet, "I don't mind."

She smiled, forgetting that she didn't make it a practice to entertain men in her home. Tonight she and Devlin were riding on a higher plane than mere physical attraction. True, there was no denying the desire that was like a burning ember, waiting to be fanned into a spark of pleasure which in turn would ignite a bursting flame of taking and giving. But at this minute, this very minute, it was a longing that transcended the physical; in Erin's heart it seemed that they walked in a beautiful, heavenly place, relishing and cherishing this oneness, savoring the total essence of the other.

"I'm going to take this gown off. I'll be back in a second."

"Take your time," he returned lazily, a grin creasing his face. "I'll enjoy seeing this meal cooked more than I'll enjoy eating it." When she lifted her brows in query, he explained, "I've never seen a naked woman cook before."

"Silly," she admonished on a smothered chuckle, color faintly rouging her cheeks. "I'll put on some jeans then. I wouldn't want to get into any strange habits."

"I've got to admit," he rejoined, his hand tightening on hers, the husky vibes giving her pleasure, "I wouldn't like for that to become a habit either." His eyes sparkled with laughter. "But I wouldn't mind if it were a habit only when you were cooking for me." Erin didn't laugh this time because his expression changed from gentle teasing to a pensive seriousness. "Let me help you undress, Erin."

"Not now," she answered, her voice low and controlled. "Maybe later . . ." Her words softly echoed into a silence that loomed between them. In the same low, clear tones she finished her statement. "Give me a little more time."

He smiled, accepting her answer. It held promise. He knew that they would develop a meaningful relationship, and he knew after that the loving would come naturally. When she tugged her hand, he released it, watching as she moved toward her bedroom.

As she opened doors and drawers, undressing and redressing in a pair of jeans and a shirt, Erin decided that an affair was just what she needed. Therapeutic! After all, it had been years since she'd gone to bed with a man. As long as she could handle the situation, why not?

Later, as she prepared dinner, Devlin watched an old movie on television starring Katherine Hepburn and Spencer Tracy. When he wasn't popping in and out of the kitchen to check on her, she would watch the movie with him. Both of them laughed and talked about the show, enjoying not so much the movie as their togetherness. Both were starved for companionship and friendship.

Of course, neither was truly aware of how lonely they were. Yet each subconsciously felt it; each consciously reacted to it. Devlin, content with satisfying his carnal needs since his wife had died, had been reluctant to get seriously involved with a woman. Because of this, he had never allowed himself really to know the women with whom he slept; he had never become friends with them.

Erin, on the other hand, thought too little of men to become friends with them. She certainly didn't like or respect them enough to take a lover, and she allowed the hatred she felt for Joe G. and Ralph to obstruct any friendship with the opposite sex. She was afraid that through friendship she might allow a man access to her intellectual and spiritual self, territory that she had denied any man.

"Have you ever noticed," Devlin mentioned at one point during the show, "that in a lot of Tracy and Hepburn movies they live separate lives, yet they're supposed to be deeply in love." He turned his head on the pillow, looking at her.

"I've thought about it," she replied.

"That's one helluva way to be married," he scathed. "If I ever marry again, you can bet your bottom dollar that my wife will live in the same house with me and share the same bed."

Erin laughed at his strong assertion. "She may prefer twin beds."

"I don't care what the size of the bed is," he retorted with a guffaw, "as long as both of us sleep in the same bed. She'll just have to decide which one is going to be *our* bed."

As he talked, Devlin's eyes strayed leisurely over Erin's face, catching the faint tinge of color, noticing the softening of the blue eyes. He thought she was more beautiful than he'd ever seen her. Curls, refusing to be tamed, escaped the chignon and hung in tendrils around her face, framing her in golden softness. Her lips, no longer glossy with lipstick, were quirked into an enigmatic smile. The shirt and the jeans were old, faded, and frayed from too many washings and gave her a vulnerable innocence. Momentarily her defenses were down, and Devlin saw the woman that few were privileged to have seen. He saw the Erin Lindsay who existed before all the hurts and bruises; e saw the little girl who was still looking for love. Moreover, he saw the woman who was looking for love.

"Would you marry a man to sleep by yourself, Erin?"

She shrugged. "I won't marry again, so there's no point in my answering a hypothetical question."

"Then let me make it less conditional. Do you think you'd enjoy sleeping with me?"

"Yes," she replied steadily, "I think I would."

His eyes took on an enigmatic glaze of their own, and amorous fires flickered in their black depths. "I'd like to sleep with you too. I know I'd enjoy it."

Letting the intimacy of the moment fade away, she stood, pulling her shirt over her hips. "I'd better check on dinner." Ignoring the faint laughter that came from the man on the sofa, she made her way to the kitchen.

Later when they ate, they laughed together, slipping into a comfortable and familiar oneness. They didn't exchange those personal intimacies like lovers do, but they were on a higher level than desultory or random conversation. They had abandoned stilted and trite remarks. Slowly, like two boxers in the ring who are sizing each other up, they circled each other, wary and contemplative, learning each other, watching and listening.

"How are you going to spend your holidays?" Devlin asked, pushing his plate aside, leaning back in his chair.

"I'll probably go to Joe G.'s," she answered indifferently.

"You don't sound too enthused about it."

"Just something to do, so I won't have to spend the day by myself."

"How about spending the day with us?"

"You and the girls?"

"All my family."

"I don't know," she murmured doubtfully, nervously stacking the dishes. "This is quite sudden."

Catching both her hands, forcing her to look up at him, he said, "No, Erin, it's not sudden. Do you want to be with us or not?"

"I don't want to intrude," she answered.

"You wouldn't be."

"Your entire family's coming down."

"No, we're going up there."

"Up where?" she asked inanely.

"Seguin. To Mother's."

"When?"

He grinned. "After work next Wednesday."

She smiled weakly. "I don't think so, Devlin. Holidays are rather personal times."

"Holidays are rather personal, but don't you think we're reaching a rather personal point in our relationship." When she didn't answer him, he added, "I think you do; otherwise, you wouldn't have agreed to see me tonight."

"Yes," she acknowledged, smiling tentatively, "we have."

"Then why can't you come meet my family?"

"It might suggest more to them than I want it to."

"You're not coming?"

"I don't know," she sighed. "Let me think about it."

"For how long?"

After I clean up the kitchen," she retorted, grinning.

"Then I'll help."

"No," she said, lifting the dishes herself. "I want plenty of time."

He gazed pensively into her face and slowly nodded. "Okay, but don't take too long." He moved to the doorway, turning to add, "You'll enjoy it, Erin. I promise."

Long after he had returned to the living room and stretched out on the sofa, Erin's soft laughter filled him with a happiness and well-being that he hadn't experienced in a long time. Soon, however, the exhaustion of the day caught up with him and by the time Erin joined him, he was asleep.

Letting him rest, she sat for a while, watching one show after the next, seeing only pictures as they flashed across the screen, paying no attention to the dialogue or the plot. Totally preoccupied with this man, she whiled away the time in thought. But as it grew later, she knew that she should awaken him.

Quietly she crept across the room, kneeling beside the sofa, gently shaking the big man who looked so peaceful in his sleep. "Devlin," she called softly, "wake up. It's late."

Slowly he lifted his heavy lids, looking at her, sleep giving his ebony eyes a warmth and intimacy she'd never noticed before. He lifted his hand from his chest and brushed it over her head, not caring that he messed up her hair.

"I'm sorry," he apologized in a husky whisper. "I didn't know I was this tired."

"I don't mind," she murmured, returning his smile, sitting on the floor, her body quivering with delight, purring her pleasure as his hand continued to fondle her hair, as his fingertips gently massaged her scalp.

"Ready for bed?"

She nodded. "I am, but I don't think you're ready for me."

His hand slid to her face, and his fingers lightly traced her mouth. "Let me stay, Erin."

"It's not the right time," she whispered.

"Yes, it is," he refuted her. "Your body's begging me to stay. Earlier it told me that you wanted to sleep with me."

"Quite possibly you misunderstood." She laughed quietly.

"I don't think so," came the equally quiet answer.

Her eyes twinkled impishly. "I do have a guest bedroom that you can use."

"I think you're the one who's misunderstanding," Devlin chuckled. "I'm not a guest—" His voice lowered. "At least, I don't want to be a guest. I want to be a permanent part of your life."

"Oh, Devlin," she sighed in exasperation, "that's what frightens me about you. You're too serious; you demand too much."

Devlin couldn't help but be disappointed by Erin's reply, but, at the same time, he recognized the sincerity of her appeal. Momentarily disregarding her utterance, his ebony eyes pierced into the blueness of hers, and he searched for the answer to his questions. Surely, he thought, she had to want more than a superficial affair; she had to desire more than just a physical coming together of two bodies.

"You're right," he drawled slowly, still looking, trying to find more than what Erin offered to him. "I want more than sex. That doesn't mean that I won't take what's offered, but I won't be satisfied with less than all of you."

He was searching for her. Erin was sure; there was no doubt. She swallowed disappointment; she swallowed a hurt that had been swelling and festering in her heart. He was searching for more than she had to give him. Possibly more than she possessed herself.

"I've been trying to tell you that I'm not ready or willing for anyone to become a permanent part of my life," she explained brokenly. "To be frank, Devlin, I don't know if I'm capable of loving someone."

If it hadn't been for the soft peal of truth that Devlin heard, he might have been angry. But he couldn't be because she didn't hide behind semantics or hypocrisy. If her explanation were subterfuge, it was unintentional on her part, and Devlin recognized this. As a result, he was disappointed, slightly irritated, but certainly not angry. Naturally he had hoped for more and had actually expected more.

"Exactly what do you want from me?" he asked curiously, his hand still playing with the soft contours of her face.

She shrugged and lowered her head, escaping the sensual caress of his fingers, escaping the hypnotic spell that he seemed to cast over her. Nervously she began to play with the buttons on the front of her shirt. "I don't know," she finally mumbled.

Devlin pursed his lips and repeated in a dangerously quiet voice. "You don't know." His face was as expressionless as the statement. Twisting a strand of her hair around his finger, he asked casually, "When will you know?"

Although Erin didn't look up, she felt his tension and his disappointment, which she mistook for anger. "Please, don't be angry," she pleaded quietly.

"I'm not," he assured her gently, pausing to lift his shoulder in an empty gesture of frustration. "I'm—well, let's just say that I'm one mass of mixed emotions at the moment." Again he hesitated. "To be frank, Erin, I don't appreciate your leading me this far to—"

"I know," she muttered contritely, breaking into his sentence. But the spitfire in her surfaced, and she lifted both her face and her voice in defiance. "But it's as much your fault as mine."

"Really?" He arched his brows skeptically, giving vent to his doubt. She nodded, and he shook his head. "I don't think so, but maybe! However, is it wrong of me to expect more tonight, Erin? Is it wrong of me to hope that what we'll share will be more than a fleeting memory for both of us? More than a casual affair?"

Erin didn't speak, only shook her head, her eyes on the button that she shoved back and forth through the buttonhole. Eventually she lifted her face and looked at him. "I've never met a man like you in my entire life, Devlin." He accepted her confession with a bland expression and in silence. He didn't so much as nod his head. "I'm very attracted to you." Her eyes softened, and she smiled her confession. "Eventually I will want to sleep with you. Still, I won't promise that it'll be more than a—" she groped for his words "—a fleeting memory. I want to make love with you, but—"

"There's always a but, isn't there? Always a condition?" He dropped the strand of hair and pushed himself into a sitting position on the sofa, swinging his feet to the floor at the same time. "You want all the giving to be on my side, Erin, and I resent it."

"What do you mean?" she exclaimed indignantly.

"You want me to open myself to you, but you refuse to do the same for me. You want me to make love to you, but you only want to make sex with me."

A moroseness tinged Devlin's words and smote Erin to the core of her being. She hurt for him, and she wanted to comfort him. But she wouldn't promise more than she felt. Just because he wanted more than a casual interlude didn't mean that she wanted more. Just because he was willing to give her so much of himself didn't guarantee that she could give that much of herself in return.

She nodded her head in agreement. "I guess you're right. I am asking more of you than I'm prepared to give. When we go to bed together, I do want you to make love to me."

Devlin studied her for a few minutes, then shook his head in puzzlement, letting the pensive silence engulf them, letting it grow heavy. Without raising his voice, he said, "If I just wanted a body, if I just wanted sex, Erin, I could easily find it. It requires little effort for a person to share his body with another." He smiled wistfully. "I tried to tell you the other day that I've had my share of empty sex and easy makes. I want more now. And I won't stop until I've found you, discovered the essence of you, until I've tasted more than the physical from you."

Erin laughed bitterly. "You don't know what you're asking, Devlin Douglas! There's nothing of me to give!" She threw her head back and glared defiantly at him. "If you knew me better, you'd be only too glad to have my body, and you'd want to avoid the inner woman at all costs. You wouldn't want me. I'm dead, Devlin. Dead and cold! I don't have any emotions left."

Devlin reached out and capped the crown of her head with the palm of his hand, his fingers splaying into her hair. "No, my darling, you're wrong. The longer I'm around you, the more I want you, the real you, the inner woman. And I won't turn you loose until I've made you mine." He chuckled. "In the meantime, I'm not going to turn down such a delectable body either."

Erin smiled, but she didn't laugh with him. "I would enjoy going to bed with you, Devlin, because I know you care." She pushed a curl from her face, tucking it behind her ear. "That's why I want you to go to bed with me," she clarified. "For the first time in my life, I would be making—making—" She struggled for her words. "For the first time in my life, a man would be making love to me because of me." She saw his frown disappear, and she saw the smile that began to radiate from his eyes. "But," she continued hurriedly, not wanting him to get his hopes up too high, "I'm afraid that my heart and soul shall have to belong only to me." Quietly, emphatically, she added, "They're mine, Devlin. All mine! And I'm afraid to share them with anyone."

"I think you're selling yourself short," Devlin retorted briefly, "and I think you're still underestimating me."

Erin shrugged. "You could be right. I don't know; however, I do know that I'm willing to accept what can be between us." She leaned against the sofa, running her finger up and down the crease of his slacks. "I also know that I'm the realist. You're the romantic. You're the one who's pushing for more than I can give all the time." She laid her face against his leg and nuzzled, feeling the muscles of his thigh as they tensed. "That's why I don't want you to make love to me until you can accept me as I am, until you quit trying to make me into something that I'm not, until you quit trying to make our affair into more than an affair."

"Trying to cure the incurable romantic?" Devlin mocked sarcastically.

Erin didn't lift her face. "No," she answered gently, "I'm just trying to give you my best." She paused. "I do think you deserve that, Devlin, and I'm prepared to be as honest with you as I can."

"Okay," he finally acquiesced after a long silence, "we'll do it your way. For the time being, I'll ask for nothing, and I'll take what I can get, angel." His tenderness and his gentleness dug and burrowed beneath her hurt and pain, filling her with a contriteness she had never felt before. "But I warn you, Erin, I shall constantly be chiseling away at your defenses. At the risk of sounding redundant and trite, I'll repeat myself. I don't need sex for sex's sake. I need and want the wellspring of you. I want some of you flowing over me, in me, all around me." His hands settled on her shoulders, and he lifted her from the floor, drawing her against the protective warmth of his body, offering her no more than solace. "And I want you to understand that I'm being patient only because both of us need love, Erin. Because both of us need each other."

"If I were capable of love," she confessed in a muffled,

broken voice, snuggling beside him on the sofa, burying her face on his shoulder, "I think I could love you." She whispered, and he almost didn't hear the faint words, "I would like to love you."

He laughed warmly, the muscles of his chest rippling, his arms binding her to him. "At least that's a beginning, little one."

"The beginning," she murmured. "Are you sure it's not the end?"

She shivered when he shook his head and his hands began to move up and down her back. She was glad that he was holding her, glad that she wasn't alone. Her heart began to thump wildly, and she was happy because he wouldn't be discouraged. She was glad because she wanted to see him again. She wanted to know him intimately. She needed to know him more intimately. Her body asked this of her, and, although she didn't realize it at the moment, her inner self demanded it of her too.

"Definitely the beginning," he affirmed. "As you requested, love, I'm going to give you more time." He laughed. "More time to fall in love with me." His words echoed his happiness. "I'm really a lovable guy, and if you're around me long enough, you'll have to give in. I'll make an incurable romantic out of you before you make a realist out of me."

"You're quite sure of yourself," she countered, a spark of defiance in her eyes.

"Very sure," he asserted with more assurance than he really felt. He leaned back, looking into her face. "Now it's time that you were tucked in bed, fast asleep." Unsuccessfully he tried to stifle a yawn. "And past time that I was in bed."

"I wish you didn't have to leave," Erin lamented softly. "I wish you'd stay longer."

"Stay to be tormented with your nearness, knowing that

I can't make love to you." He laughed. "I'm afraid, Erin, I've had about all I can take tonight."

"Oh, Devlin," she murmured, wanting him to stay, yet wanting him to go.

He pulled her closer to him and shushed her. "Have you thought about going home with me for Thanksgiving?"

"Are you sure your family wouldn't mind?"

"They won't," he assured her, "and I want you to go." *It's time that you meet some real people, Erin, he thought, people who aren't afraid of showing their feelings. Of loving, of being loved.*

"When would we leave?"

"Wednesday after work."

"Are the girls going with us?"

He shook his head. "No, they're flying down Friday after school." He grinned when he saw the question in her eyes. "The private school they attend is closed for the entire Thanksgiving week. So they're going down early, but they'll come back with us Saturday."

"What if you get tired of me before Saturday?" she quizzed.

"Feed you to the buzzards."

"Thanks!" She grimaced.

"But, remember," he pointed out, "I'll only do that if I get tired of you." He grinned. "I'm not going to tell you what I'm going to do if you please me."

"Threats or promises?" she teased.

"Sweet promises, darling. Sweet promises."

Serious again, she asked, "What if the girls don't like me?"

"The girls will like you," he assured her, "but if they don't, Erin, I'll bring you home sooner. I won't let you be hurt, darling."

"Oh, Devlin," she exclaimed, snuggling up to him. "Are you sure this is going to be all right?"

"I'm sure," he answered softly.

She ran her finger around his collar. "Let's wait. Maybe by Christmas . . ."

He moved, and his hands cupped her face, his lips gently trailing kisses from her eyes to her mouth. "No." His denial was firm. "I'll agree to wait before I make love to you, but I insist on this weekend with my family. I want you with me for Thanksgiving."

"I just have this feeling."

"Trust me," he said. "I wouldn't ask you to do something that would be hurtful or harmful for you."

"It's not that," she countered.

"You've got to be willing to take a chance, Erin."

"Okay," she whispered, but he could still hear her doubt and hesitancy. He understood her fear.

"We'll take it a day at a time."

She nodded, lifting her face, closing her eyes, savoring the feel of his mouth as it caressed her cheeks. Then his lips covered hers, soft and appealing as he tipped his head to the side and moved it in lazy, seductive motions back and forth, sending tiny shudders up her arms and fluid fire through her veins. His tongue, warm and gentle, outlined her mouth, and her lips parted to answer his tongue. The warm kiss turned into a burning hotness, growing wilder, more intimate as Devlin's soft, sensual lips melted her resistance, making her vitally aware of her emptiness and her loneliness. He lifted his lips and gazed, starry-eyed into her face.

"Dear God, Erin, you don't know how badly I want to stay." He barely held his emotions in check. His entire body ached for her.

"You promised to give both of us more time," Erin reminded him gently.

Breathing deeply, he moved and withdrew his arms from around her. Leaning forward, he muttered, "So I did." He raked his hands through his hair, then pushed himself to his feet, and stood. "Okay, sweetheart, I'll give you a little more time. But that's all. Just a l-i-t-t-l-e—" he spelled the word for emphasis "—more time." He picked up his vest and tie, draping them over his arm. "Tonight I'm going home, and I know I'm going to regret having done it. The next time, Erin, we'll sleep together." His voice died, but his promise, vibrantly alive, rang deeply and loudly in Erin's heart.

CHAPTER SIX

Erin stepped out of the warm shower onto the blue bath-mat, hurriedly drying herself, so the girls could use the bath. Wringing out the washcloth, she draped it and the towel over the rack before she slipped into her cotton robe, zipping up the front. With quick, jerky movements, she picked up her soiled clothes and padded to the bedroom that she'd been sharing with Nanette and Devalind for the past two nights. She smiled as her hand clasped the door-knob. If the house hadn't been so crowded with the Douglas family, she would have thought there was an ulterior scheme behind the sleeping arrangement.

"I'm through with the bathroom," she announced as she pushed on the door and stepped into the large, country-style bedroom with its pastel-colored gingham curtains and matching bedspreads. The pinks and light greens reflected the bright gaiety of the two girls who claimed the room as their own.

"You took so long that I used Grandma's bath," came the frank reply from the twelve-year-old who was reading her latest mystery novel. She sprawled across the floor, half-propping herself on a monstrous, red beanbag chair that clashed horribly with the delicate white provincial furniture and the pastel accessories.

"Me too," eight-year-old Nanette chimed in as she brushed her long brown hair. She primped a little longer in front of the dresser before she said, "I just need to fix my hair, and I'm ready to go."

Erin walked to one of the twin beds, pulling her suitcase from beneath it. "Are you sure you bathed?" she grunted, flopping it on the bed, "or did you just get wet?"

"I bathed," Nanette replied quickly, watching Erin as she put her soiled clothes in a small plastic bag. "But, remember, I'm smaller than you are, so it doesn't take me as long." Her deeply blue eyes glimmered with saucy amusement, and she giggled when Erin looked up to glower in her direction. "We had to hurry, Erin, Uncle Charles is going to leave early, and we're going with him." Nanette laid the brush on the dresser and walked to the bed across from Erin, unceremoniously hopping to the middle of the gingham spread. "Uncle Charles is our newest uncle," she explained. "He married Aunt Shirley last Valentine's. Me and Lindy were in the wedding." She turned to peer at Devalind. "Weren't we, Lindy?" Devalind responded with a grunt, which Nanette accepted as an affirmative answer. "Now all Daddy's brothers and sisters are married." She smiled wickedly. "Except Daddy." Again she giggled. "And he's the only one with kids."

"Aunt Patsy's pregnant," Devalind reminded her sister.

"Well," Nanette hissed waspishly, "she still hasn't got it here yet, so it doesn't count."

Temporarily disconcerted, Nanette devoted all her attention to putting her socks and shoes on. Then she tucked her feet under her, sitting cross-legged on the bed. "Uncle Charles is gonna let us get a hamburger on the way, and, boy, am I glad." She patted her stomach. "I've eaten so much turkey in the last two days I think I can gobble better than he can."

Devalind's full attention rested on her sister. "I don't know if you can gobble as well as he can," she interjected dryly, sounding like a miniature Devlin, "but you're certainly beginning to look like one."

"Whata ya mean by that?" Nanette demanded defensively, a glimmer of anger in her voice.

"You're getting fat, and you waddle just like a turkey."

"Gag you!" Nanette hissed back. "And furthermore it's not as fat as a turkey. It's as fat as a pig, and—" Her voice grew more assertive and saucy. She looked at Erin, who was standing by the bed, getting her clean underwear from the suitcase. "Do you think I waddle like a turkey, Erin?"

"I think one always says, strut like a turkey, Nanette, and waddle like a duck." Erin's face was a mirror of amusement.

"See there!" Nanette flung at Devalind. "You were wrong altogether. Turkeys don't waddle."

"But you do," Devalind mocked with a lilting laugh.

"Do I, Erin?" Nanette wailed. "Do I waddle? Am I getting fat?"

Erin chuckled, pressing the lock on the suitcase. "No, Netty," she replied, unconsciously and naturally using the diminutive that the family had lovingly applied to the younger Douglas child. "You don't waddle, and you're not fat. Your sister is just teasing you."

"Were you, Lindy?" Nanette demanded in an injured tone, playing the wounded victim to the hilt. "Were you just teasing me?"

Devalind continued to stare at her sister, refusing to answer immediately. Finally, however, after Nanette repeated her question several times, her voice getting louder and more demanding, Devalind's serious face was split by a smile that slowly fanned from her mouth to her eyes. So much like Devlin, Erin thought with a catch of her breath. Not in looks so much, but in actions. That dry sense of humor. That deep undercurrent of love and affection.

Devalind began to nod her head. "I was joking, Netty. You're not fat, and you don't waddle." She caught one corner of her bottom lip with her teeth and murmured, "You're gonna look just like Mother. You're gonna be beautiful."

Excitedly Nanette jumped on her knees and crawled to the end of the bed, peering downward into Devalind's face. "You think so?" she demanded as if Devalind were truth personified, speaking to her. "Do you really think so, Lindy?"

Devalind smiled, and Erin could see the sadness that tinged the blue eyes. "Not only are you going to look like her, Netty, you also do things that make me think of her."

Erin could hear the loneliness that threaded the child's words; she could feel that desolation that comes to a person when she remembers a particularly painful moment. Erin identified with Devalind; she remembered the grief and sorrow; she remembered the aloneness. She wanted to go to Devalind, to wrap her arms around her, to love her. But she knew this wasn't the appropriate time. She hadn't known Devalind long enough to do that. She must, therefore, give the child comfort in the form of words.

Softly she said, "Odd, that you would say that, Lindy. I was just standing here thinking how much you remind me of your father."

Devalind flipped over, propped up on one elbow, and pulled a surprised face. "You really think so?" she asked quietly, pushing a brown fringe of hair off her forehead.

Erin nodded. "I do think so! You do things that remind me of him, just like Netty does things that remind you of your mother."

Devalind picked at one of the huge buttons on the beanbag. "But I don't look like Mother or Daddy. I'm not pretty, and both of them are. Mother was beautiful, and Daddy's handsome."

"Beauty isn't on the outside, Lindy," Erin explained on

a soft note. "Beauty is of the soul; it's a reflection of your inner self. Beauty is caring; it's loving; it's trust and truth. Beauty is gentleness and tenderness."

"Golly, Erin," Nanette exploded in a coarse whisper, "you preach better than Pastor Haydon, and you're not dull and boring." Her eyes were wide, opened circles.

Erin felt a warm happiness as it slowly effused through her body, and it took the sound of beautiful laughter, the song of the soul. "I don't think I'm cut out to be a preacher, Netty, but I'm glad you think I speak as well as Pastor Haydon. I was spellbound with his sermon at the Thanksgiving service."

Nanette giggled, finally collapsing on the bed, racked with spasms. "I didn't think you heard him, the way you and Daddy held hands and grinned at each other through church."

Erin's face softly fused with color. "Netty!" she murmured. "Your father and I did not behave like that."

The child guffawed now. "Oh, yes, you did! Me and Lindy watched you. We even punched Grandma, so she could see too." She caught her breath. "Daddy played with your fingers, and then he—"

Devalind's quiet chuckle interrupted Nanette. "On the way home from church when Grandpa thought we weren't listening he told Grandma that Daddy hadn't been to church at all. He said Daddy had one thing on his mind."

Erin's eyes flew open, her mouth dropped, and her face turned a deep shade of red. She couldn't have replied if she had wanted to. She was speechless.

"And we know what that one thing was," Nanette chimed in with a snicker. "Daddy had you on his mind."

To cover her embarrassment Erin busied herself with straightening the creases out of the bedspread. She flipped the throw pillows a time or two, and she breathed deeply, relieved with Netty's last declaration.

"Erin," Devalind called softly.

Erin turned to catch the child studying her. "Yes."

"Do you like my daddy?"

Though a simple question, Erin understood all the meanings. She meticulously folded her underwear, lying it on the foot of the bed, and she walked to the dresser. Not having expected the sudden turn in the conversation, she was more than disconcerted. Out of habit her hand went to the tassle hanging from the zipper of her robe, and she pulled it through her fingers as she mulled the fullness of her answer.

Eventually she said, "I like your father."

"Really like him," the child persisted, not satisfied with Erin's answer.

There was just a slight pause before Erin replied. "I really like him."

How could she explain to the children that her definition of like and their definition was different. How could she tell them that she wanted to know their daddy better but that she didn't want to know him too well. How could she tell them that she was frightened of commitments.

Nanette didn't seem to notice Erin's quietness, and she accepted the reply at face value. "Daddy likes you too," she proclaimed with that innate wisdom and insight that belongs only to a child.

Erin lifted the brush to her hair, pulling it through the thick blond waves. "What makes you think so?" she asked.

Nanette watched as Erin brushed carefully. "I just know," she replied with a shrug. "The way he laughs, for one thing," she said quietly, more subdued than Erin had seen her during the past two days. "He hasn't laughed like that since Mother died." Simply stated, her words held no rancor or jealousy. She continued. "He laughs with me and Lindy, but not the way he laughed with Mother or the way he laughs with you."

At a loss for words—the right words—Erin asked, "Do you mind?"

"At first I did," Nanette responded with her natural honesty, "but I don't know now." She thought for a second, screwing her face up. "I . . . don't think so." She flipped on the bed and grinned at Erin's reflection in the mirror. "Probably I won't mind as long as he loves me and Lindy."

Erin smiled and felt a knot as it slowly insinuated itself in her heart. She blinked back the tears, understanding the child's fears. She understood all her doubts and questions. Slowly she swallowed, striving for a nonchalance she was far from feeling.

"Your father's liking me and my liking him will never interfere with his love for you." She laid the brush down and began to absently pick up, one by one, the bottles of perfume on the dresser. "He could hardly wait for the holidays to be with you." She smiled. "He said that it felt like years instead of days since he'd seen you. And he showed me all kinds of photos and talked about his two beautiful girls constantly." She looked first at Nanette, then down at Devalind. "He wanted me to come spend Thanksgiving with you so I could meet you. He's very proud of you."

"We're proud of him too," Devalind chimed in. She smiled, and although she wasn't beautiful, Erin knew as she grew older she would never have any trouble attracting men. Her blue eyes sparkled with the adventure of life, and her smile radiated with love, mirroring the fire of her personality. "You're not so bad yourself, Erin!"

"No, you're not!" Nanette exclaimed with heated feeling. "I'd say on a scale of one to ten, you're—" she stopped talking, thought a minute, cocked a saucy eye at Erin, and said "—I'd say you're a ten plus."

Simultaneously the three of them began to laugh, and the final cord of tension broke. "Thank you, Netty," Erin finally gasped, "I really appreciate that. I don't quite see myself as a ten plus, but I'd like to think I am. Now, I'll have to add that I think the two of you are something else too." She paused, drew a deep breath, and expelled it slowly. "You're . . . the . . . *greatest!*"

Nanette grinned and flopped to a sitting position, reaching for the candy bar on her nightstand. Quite meticulously she peeled off the wrapper and carefully inspected the end before she bit into it. "Well, if you want to know the truth," she divulged, taking her first tentative bite of the chocolate bar, "when Daddy called to tell Grandma that he was bringing you home for the holidays, Lindy and I weren't too happy." She took another bite of the candy, chewed, and swallowed before she said, "But, Grandma—" She grinned and threw her hands up in loving exasperation. "She was all smiles." Netty looked at Devalind, and both of them giggled. "What does she look like, Devy?" Nanette mimicked, screwing her face up like her grandmother. "How old is she, Devy? Are you serious about her, Devy? I can hardly wait, Devy?"

Despite herself, Erin couldn't help but laugh at the way Nanette mimicked her grandmother.

"Remember, Lindy?" Nanette added. "Girls, this is just what your daddy needs—a woman in his life."

"Netty," Devalind reprimanded softly, "don't get carried away."

Totally unperturbed, basking in the warmth of her confession, Nanette took another bite of the candy, and glowered her disapproval at Devalind. "Well, Lindy, it's the truth. That's what Grandma said. And, furthermore," she continued with a snippy gait to her words, "we didn't want her to come." She looked at Erin and grinned sheepishly. "When Grandma was figuring out who was going to sleep where, we got angry because she said you were gonna hafta share our room with us."

"Nanette Douglas!" Devalind barked sharply, jackknifing into a sitting position. "You'd better hush up before you get yourself into trouble!"

Nanette shook her head, her eyes glaring defiantly at Devalind before they riveted back to Erin. "But it's true, Lindy, neither one of us wanted to share our room with Erin."

Although the child's confession hurt Erin, she could understand their feelings. To them she was an intruder, a stranger who had barged in on their holiday.

"Would you like for me to move?" she asked quietly. "Now that your aunts and uncles are gone, I could ask your grandmother to move me to another bedroom."

"Oh, no!" Devalind bellowed quickly. "Don't move, Erin. Please stay in here with us." She pleaded on a soft note. "We like you now, and we want you to stay in our bedroom."

Not knowing that her confession had brought about Erin's mollifying gesture, Nanette's face blanched white, and she wailed, "Don't move, Erin." Her eyes were large circles in her pale face, and her candy bar was suspended in midair. "That's the way we felt before we met you." She grinned, holding the half-eaten bar of candy to Erin. "Now we like you." She stretched her arm a little farther out. "You want a bite. It's real good." Not a candy enthusiast, Erin didn't immediately reach out. "Go ahead," Nanette insisted, "have a bite."

"I—I don't want to eat your candy," Erin finally said, not understanding that this was a conciliatory action on Nanette's part.

"We really like you," Nanette said, a doleful pleading in her voice. "Really we do." Her blue eyes fell from Erin's face to the partially eaten chocolate.

Devalind smiled. "Netty doesn't share her candy bars with just anyone, Erin. Just special people!"

Erin looked from one child to the other, and she listened to Devalind. But she heard Nanette's heart-cry and intuitively knew she had to take a bite of the candy. She lifted the bar to her mouth. "Thanks, Netty." She grinned, a splinter of chocolate on the corner of her mouth. "And you should feel privileged, too, because I don't eat just anybody's candy." She slowly chewed her small bite and swallowed, then said as she handed the bar back to Nanette, "Thanks for the treat." Her blue eyes softened and sparkled with a mist of tears. "More especially, thanks for liking me."

Her eyes glinted with laughter and life. "I'm glad that you're going roller-skating with us this afternoon." She darted Devalind a furtive glance and said, "We thought you were going to be an old fuddy-duddy." When Devalind gasped with outrage, Nanette nodded her head, furiously asserting, "Yes, we did, Lindy. Both of us wondered what she'd be like, and we were worried."

Erin threw her head back and began to laugh, moving across the room to wrap her arms around the younger child. With a natural warmth, a spontaneous loving she hadn't felt since her mother died, Erin hugged Nanette and laughed with her, enjoying the familial intimacy, the sharing, the caring.

"I can imagine how you felt," she confessed on a soft note. "I was afraid of meeting you too. I thought maybe the two of you were old—" She left the sentence dangling, lifted her brows, and made a face at both girls.

"No!" Devalind shrieked on stifled laughter. When Erin solemnly nodded her head, Devalind said incredulously, "You thought we were going to be old fuddy-duddies too? You were as scared of meeting us as we were of meeting you?"

Erin nodded her head, not saying a word, the three of them laughing, communicating with emotions and gestures at the moment, needing no words. When Devlin walked into the room later, he found the three of them, sitting cross-legged on the floor, talking and laughing together.

His ebony eyes feasted on the beauty of the harmonious scene. He looked first at one then the other of his daughters, seeing a different kind of happiness on their faces. He looked at Erin to see the peace and serenity that smoothed the harshness from her countenance, that softened her voice, that endowed her with a maternal beauty.

He eased his large frame in between Nanette and Devalind, putting an arm around each girl's shoulder. "What are the three of you snickering about?" he teased. "When I walked into the house, I could hear your giggling all the way in the living room."

Devalind grinned. "It's a secret, Daddy." Her face swiveled, and she winked at Erin. "A secret among us girls."

"Hmmm," Devlin droned thoughtfully, his eyes sparkling with laughter. "I don't know if I trust you girls with secrets or not. How do I know they're not about me."

"Oh, Daddy," Nanette squealed. "You can trust us to have good secrets. We were just talking—"

She got no further with her sentence because Devalind lunged across Devlin's lap and put her hands over her sister's mouth. "Oh, no, you don't!" she gasped, fighting with the squirming Nanette. "Not this time. We're keeping our little conversation to ourselves." She giggled. "Do you understand, chatterbox?"

Nanette emitted a muffled sound and began to vigorously nod her head. When Devalind made up her mind about something, Nanette knew she could be quite obstinate. And no one knew this any better than she. "Umm-hmm," she continued to thrum, but still Devalind didn't turn her loose.

Finally Devlin caught Devalind's shoulders in both hands and pulled her away from Nanette. "Not only is this a secret among you three. I think it's got to be a conspiracy against me."

"No, Daddy," Devalind protested, "it's not a secret about you. It's—"

"It's a secret which we three women want to share for a little while," Erin interrupted smoothly, pulling Devalind out of Devlin's loose grip. "It's idle woman's talk which wouldn't interest you." Her eyes flitted to the quiet Nanette, and she grinned. "However, I would imagine that before the sun rises on another day, you'll have the full details."

Devlin chuckled and fondly wrapped the small bundle of femininity in his arms. "Netty, don't let them put you down, girl. We don't mind having one blabbermouth in the family."

All of them laughed and talked until a car horn sounded a couple of times. Nanette and Devalind looked at each other with surprise, then jumped to their feet, running to the large closet that spanned the entire width of one wall.

"That's Uncle Charles," Nanette explained as they rummaged around, looking for their skates. "And you know how he hates to wait."

"Why weren't you ready then?" Devlin asked dryly. "Both of you were told that he'd be by to pick you up."

"We got to talking," Devalind said with a quick glance at Erin, "and we forgot all about the time." When the horn blared a third and fourth time, the girls ran from the room. Just outside the door Devalind stopped and turned. "Daddy, you and Erin are going to meet us there, aren't you?"

Devlin smiled. "We'll meet you there."

"Promise!" She looked directly into Erin's face.

"Promise!" Erin rejoined.

After the girls shut the door, Devlin scooted across the floor and reached for Erin, pulling her into his arms.

"Ummm," he sighed, "this feels good. I love holding my girls. First my little ones, now my bigger one."

Erin pressed her face into the softness of his velour shirt, feeling the latent strength and the urgency of his hard, powerful grasp. She felt the tautness of his body; she heard the heavy thumps of his heart. Gloriously intoxicated by his masculine odor, Erin breathed deeply and chuckled.

"I don't know whether I'm flattered or insulted."

"You should definitely be flattered, my dear lady."

He lifted one big hand—a strong hand, a gentle hand—and tipped her chin up to kiss her lips softly. Erin's hands at the same time slid up his chest, locking behind his neck, her fingers barely touching the crisp black hair at the base of his neck.

"Thank you, then, Mr. Douglas," she murmured faintly, as he moved himself slightly, as he caught her closer to him, as he deepened the kiss.

Cooperating fully, her mouth opened beneath his, and she felt the pounding of his heart through her robe. It was a long, slow, searching kiss, and when he finally lifted his head, Erin brought it down again, greedily opening her mouth for a second kiss which lasted even longer than the first one.

"What sweet torment," Devlin said when finally they broke apart. "If only you knew how much you move me, little angel."

"You move me too," she whispered.

"If only you knew how much I want to make love to you."

"I want to make love to you too." There was no hesitancy in her words, no reticence.

"Oh, baby," he groaned, "you are tearing me apart." His lips trailed paths of fire across her cheeks, to her ears, down the slender column of her throat. Softly he asked, "Do you really want to make love to me?"

"I'm still a coward at heart," she warned him. "And I'm saying no more than what you hear. Please don't read between the lines, because there's nothing to read."

"I don't make it a habit to read between the lines," he murmured, his warm breath seductively whispering over her sensitive skin. "But I do read you, and I'll warn you right now your cowardice is rather short-lived."

"More of those idle threats," Erin gibed, running her fingers through the thick hair at the base of his neck, pulling back to peer innocently into his face.

"No more idle threats," he promised. "No more waiting either."

Erin grinned. "A little more waiting," she pointed out. "The traffic is a little too heavy in this house."

Devlin chuckled. "If only you knew what was in store for you, woman, you wouldn't want to wait another minute, traffic or not."

Erin shivered with anticipation, feeling the white-hot flames of his love as they penetrated through her thin robe, through her façade of indifference. She felt their burning sting; she felt the branding touch as he marked her for himself. She lifted her face, hungry again for the touch of his lips, murmuring, "Maybe you're right."

"Oh, God," he groaned, lowering his face, his lips touching hers, gently moving back and forth, his tongue gently pressuring into the sweet loveliness of her mouth. "What a time to tell me."

Just as the kiss began to deepen, just as Devlin's hands began a more thorough exploration of the sensual terrain of Erin's body, they heard Nanette shout as she barged through the front door.

"We had to come back, Daddy. We forgot to get any money."

Devlin rolled away from Erin, uttering expletives under his breath. As Erin hurriedly straightened her robe, he raked his hand through his hair, mussing it even more. "If it's not one thing, it's another."

Erin laughed. "I told you there was too much traffic here."

He glowered at her. "There's nothing funny to laugh about." Slowly he levered himself to his feet, holding out his hand, grasping her outstretched one. "You'd better get dressed," he instructed her in a voice still hoarse from their lovemaking, "or you'll get more than you bargained for, thoroughfare or not."

Breathlessly she landed against his chest, placing her hands palm forward. She lifted her face to his, the laughter still dancing in her eyes, happiness shining on her entire countenance.

"You don't know what I'm bargaining for," she tormented in a soft voice. Her mouth curved into a beautiful smile, seductively alluring. "No idea at all, Devlin Douglas."

It was the beauty and the warmth of her soul that touched Devlin, that reached him. And without her knowing it she branded him too; she totally possessed him. He could hardly wait for her to reveal herself totally to him, to allow him to fully know the woman she had hidden from the world for years. True, he had seen her daily discard more and more of her veneer, and she was slowly breaking out of her prison of isolation. But, still, there was so much more for him to see, to hear, to touch, to learn. He could hardly wait.

"Daddy," Nanette called again. "Did you hear me? Lindy and I need some money." Her voice was nearer this time.

Devlin clasped Erin by the shoulders and gently moved her away. "You distract me, woman, and my child who is in desperate need is summoning me."

"Perhaps you'd better reconsider having me a permanent fixture in your life."

He grinned, shaking his head forcefully. "As Netty would so delicately say, no way!" He turned and walked through the doorway. "Dad ran Mother over to Shirley's, so they can get things ready for tonight. When he returns, we'll leave."

"Daddy!" Nanette grumbled. "What took you so long!"

"How much do you think you'll need?" he asked, closing the door behind him.

In a happy daze Erin unzipped her robe and stepped out of it, throwing it across the foot of the bed. Leisurely she dressed for her afternoon at the skating rink—her designer jeans; the striped sweater in crayon-bright colors—blue, yellow, red, and green; the bright red plastic bangles, and the matching earrings. She started to catch her hair in the usual chignon of curls, but changed her mind, letting it hang loose, securing it behind her ears with two of Devalind's brightly colored barrettes.

When she was ready she draped her marigold yellow cardigan over her shoulders, tying the sleeves around her neck. She wasn't cold now, but she knew how brisk and cool November afternoons and evenings could be once the sun had gone done.

Stepping back, she checked her appearance in front of the mirror that was attached to the closet door. Last, she smiled at herself, wishing Devlin were already by her side, wishing she could share her joy and anticipation with him.

No sooner had the wish cascaded through her mind than the main persona of her dreams materialized. Dressed in charcoal gray slacks, a white turtleneck sweater, and a black leather jacket, he lounged indolently in the doorframe. His hair, brushed back from his face, fanned across part of his forehead in loose, thick waves. His eyes, as black as his hair, smiled appreciatively, raking in minute detail over the woman standing in front of the mirror.

He held his hand out as she walked across the room,

dropping her hand into his. "I'll never get over how pretty you are," he told her. "No matter what you wear, no matter how dressed up or dressed down you may be, you're still beautiful." His eyes, hot, smoldering embers of desire, flicked over her hair. His smile widened, and he softly chuckled. "No sedate little twist?" He noticed the barrettes. "My! My!" he exclaimed on bated breath. "How much you've departed from your image, Madame President."

She laughed with him. "You're having a bad influence on me."

He shook his head, his lips twitching with amusement. "No, I'm having a good influence on you. You're beginning to react like a person instead of a machine."

Not liking this feeling of vulnerability, this pregnability, Erin retaliated with, "Maybe I'm not departing from my image. Maybe you just had me pictured differently."

"Maybe," he breathed, his arms surrounding her body, his hands locking in the middle of her back. "But I don't think so."

"Still, you don't know everything," she whispered, moving closer and closer to him in graceful slow motion.

She gave up her resistance and lost herself to the magic of the moment, to the magic of the man. For years she had denied herself this; for years she had denied herself any emotion except hate. Now she was slowly opening at the command of this man as if he were the sun, she the flower in the field. It wasn't that she couldn't do without him; she didn't want to do without him.

Although she thirsted for the dewy freshness of the morning, although she longed for the soft spring rain, although she panted for the coolness of the evening, she wanted even more the hot, searing love of Devlin Douglas, the sun of her universe. She wanted to feel the heat of his emotions as they penetrated her heart, as they exchanged love for hatred, joy for bitterness. He had touched her soul. Just a small touch, she thought, that's all it took. She was branded for life. She carried Devlin Douglas's loving brand, and she could never escape.

"Tell me, Devlin Douglas," she murmured, "do you know all things?"

"No, sweetheart," he tenderly agreed, "I don't know all things. But I do know that I've never pictured you any different from what you really are. I've known from the first minute I set eyes on you that you were a woman who wanted to be loved." His hands gently nudged her back, and she rested her face against the soft material of his sweater and jacket. "Seeing you with the girls today confirmed all I felt about you. I know you're the woman I want to love." He held her tightly, almost hurting with the intensity of his love.

Erin lifted her head and pulled away from Devlin, looking into his face, viewing the emotions as they saturated his countenance. She knew that she cared for him, but still she wasn't sure that she could give him what he was asking for. She didn't know if her feeling could be defined as love. She really doubted at the moment that it was more than a purely physical desire.

"Give me a chance, Erin, to prove to you that we're meant for each other. Give me a chance to prove to you that we can love each other in a lasting way." He was asking for more than a chance. He was asking for a lifetime; he figured that he would need that long at least to study her at close range. And even with a lifetime, Devlin wasn't sure that it would be long enough for him to know her.

"Okay," she said, surrendering to the strength of his love. "I'll give myself the chance. I'm just worried about you. You're asking for so much, Devlin. So very much."

Devlin's hand tangled in her thick curls, and he pulled her face back, looking squarely into those candid blue eyes. "How can you say that?" he asked gruffly. "How come you continually sell yourself short, Erin? You're not truly giving yourself a chance. You're just spouting words to convince me—" He lapsed into silence, the sable-colored eyes penetrating the blue depth of Erin's. Slowly he resumed speaking, "Or . . . maybe . . . to . . . convince . . . yourself."

"I'm not selling myself short," Erin defended herself quietly, her voice low. "I'm just not sure that I won't be selling you short, and I've got to be sure, Devlin." Her eyes misted over with tears. "And you're wrong. I am going to give myself a chance. Truly I am," she ended on a hoarse whisper. "I'm going to give you the chance you're asking for."

Devlin's face lowered, and his lips closed over hers, pressing, searching, questing. His lovemaking was intense, verging on violence, yet he didn't frighten Erin. Rather, she responded to this primeval urge, this demanding of their flesh. Her hands twined in the crispness of his thick black hair, and his hands, starting at her waist, slid under her sweater, up the midriff to cup the fullness of her breasts which were enveloped in a lacy bra. As his fingers gently stimulated the nipples into tautness, the satiny swells burgeoned into tightness, aching for more than the touch of his hands, aching for the moist warmness of his mouth. All the while his lips were trailing paths of molten desire—golden, pure, radiant—from her lips to the center column of her neck.

"Oh, God, Erin," he said huskily, gasping in deep gulps of air, his face resting in that delightful scented curve of neck and shoulder, "these past few days have been some of the loveliest I've spent in a long, long time, but they've also been some of the most tormenting." He lifted his head, and his lips, warmly moist, trailed across her throat to find the tender curving of her ear just above the small red earring. He nibbled the sensitive skin until Erin moaned softly against his chest. "You taste so good," he whispered. "You feel so good, darling. Tell me—" his lips hovered above her ear, his breath blowing against the aroused nerve-endings of her neck "—do I feel good to you. Do I taste good to you?"

Mutely Erin nodded her head again, her hands running up and down the lapel of his jacket.

"Show me," he commanded. "Show me, my little angel."

Erin tilted her head back and looked up into his face, her eyes dilated and dazed with passion. Her hands fell slowly to his waist, her fingers deftly pulling his sweater from the waistband of his slacks. Gently, teasingly, her fingertips flew upward, and she gloried in her prowess as a lover when he sucked in his breath, when his stomach muscles tensed and tightened.

She lifted the sweater, lowered her face, and with her tongue began to stimulate his nipples. With the wet tip she circled around and around the pleasure point until Devlin grasped her face with both hands and pulled her face up to his, again capturing her lips with his.

He leaned back against the doorframe, supporting himself, pulling Erin against the full length of his hard strength, letting her feel the extent of his arousal. "I've got to have more than this, Erin. I'm hungry for you; I'm thirsty for you. And simple necking isn't good enough."

The words dropped into the musky cavern of her mouth as Devlin's lips moved seductively over them. Then his lips swept across the flushed cheeks back to the lips, covering them again in a wet, opened-mouth kiss that blatantly heralded his needs. This time his desire ran unchecked, and his mouth made love to her with an intensity and passion that almost overwhelmed her. His hands slid to her rounded bottom, and he pulled her closer to him, arched, acquainting her with his body. She groaned as she felt desire—hot, burning, unleashed—flame through her body. Her very soul was inundated with the fierceness of Devlin's love.

"I can't hardly wait to get you home," Devlin softly murmured in her ear after a long, long while, "and into my bed."

"But it's more than just going to bed, isn't it?" Erin cried desperately. "You do care, don't you, Devlin? Really care about me?"

Quite suddenly Devlin's mouth stopped moving against her ear, her neck, her cheek. His hands dropped from her hips, and he breathed deeply for a while. Gently, like a parent dressing a child, he straightened her sweater, pushed some of the stray curls away from her face, and cupped her face with both hands. Unable to meet his penetrating gaze, she closed her eyes.

"Open your eyes, Erin." The command was that given to a child who had greatly disappointed.

She shook her head, trying to pull it out of his grasp, but he refused to let her move.

"Open your eyes, sweetheart." Now he spoke to his love. "I want you to see me. I want to see you."

This command she obeyed because she knew he was speaking to her heart. Slowly her lids fluttered up, and she stared into his face, open, vulnerable, wistful. His words, soft and velvet, had touched her soul, softly rubbing away the tarnish of bitterness and anger, rubbing away all resistance, polishing her desire to a shining finish. His voice, deep and husky from sexual desire which he could not and did not try to hide from her, attempted to eradicate all doubt and question.

"Please see me, darling." The words were prayer-soft.

Erin smiled softly. "I do see you."

Sadly he shook his head. "No, little angel, I don't think you can see me yet."

"I do," Erin insisted firmly, a thread of frustration in her reply.

He continued to shake his head, his fingers teasing her temples. "No, you're only looking at me. If you saw me, Erin, really saw me, you'd trust me; you'd believe in me. You'd love me."

"I'm trying, Devlin," she murmured, her voice barely audible. "I want to see you. It's just that—" She drew a shaky breath before she could conclude her sentence. "To have your love, I have to give up so much; I have to make an unconditional surrender." She shuddered from the intensity of her feelings; she shivered as she bared herself and her fears to Devlin.

"You've got it all wrong," he corrected her, his voice almost a thrum, dull and throbbing with pain. "Loving isn't surrendering, sweetheart, and it's not devastating. It's conquering, and it's beautiful. It's the combining of two forces, two great energies to create one that's even greater. The beauty of love, the mystery of love, is that each individual, each partner, keeps his personality. Each one complements the other."

"Perhaps you're right," she acquiesced. "I really don't know. The only love I've experienced is that which I felt for my mother, and it's an entirely different kind of love from what you're asking for." She raised her hands and covered Devlin's, pressing his fingers into the burning flesh of her cheeks. "I don't know if I'd even recognize love if I saw it. From my experience—"

"That's just it," he interrupted her, shaking his head. "You don't have any experience in love. You don't know what it's like, or what it's all about. But I want to teach you, to guide you. You can't make a judgment until you've tried it, Erin."

"I—" she licked her dry lips "—won't enter into a second loveless marriage, Devlin, and I don't think you could settle for a . . . a casual affair."

Devlin laughed. "Believe me, darling girl, any affair that the two of us share will be anything but casual."

"I've never had an affair," she confessed softly. "I've never met a man whom I've really wanted to go to bed with."

"Now you're willing to have one with me?"

Erin nodded her head. "Are you willing to accept that?"

"I told you I'd take what I can get, but that doesn't mean that I'll be satisfied with it. I don't want a casual affair as such. I want marriage."

"I admit that I desire you, Devlin, but I'm not sure that it's more than desire. And I'm not willing to commit myself until I'm very sure."

"We can build a good marriage on what we feel for each other, Erin. I know we can. During the next few weeks, I'll convince you that we can."

"Tell me, Devlin, what happens when the desire dies?" she replied, weighing her words carefully. "When the like doesn't turn into love?"

Devlin's voice dropped to a rough whisper. "I can't answer that one, honey." His thumbs, tenderly running over the fullness of her bottom lip, played havoc with Erin's senses. "But I do know this. What I feel for you will never die. Also I happen to believe that the only emotion you may have possibly felt for your ex-husband—" he couldn't force himself to use Ralph's name "—was like, possibly pity, certainly not desire."

She licked her lips, mesmerized by the eyes that darkened even more with emotion. "I don't know," she murmured inanely, not following his thoughts, seeing only the tenderness and love that brightly burned there. She wanted to believe him; she wanted to trust him. But she couldn't. Not yet!

"You do know," he contradicted gruffly. "You just won't admit it. Foolishly you hide behind your fears, denying both of us the pleasure that we can share with each other." His voice hardened, and his arms, with a determined savageness, wrapped around her, and he jerked her close to his body. "It's time, Erin, to dispense with talking. I'm done with it. It's time that I showed you just what we do mean to each other. It's time that I overrode those stupid ideas of yours." Giving up the argument, he resorted to the only language he thought Erin would understand, to which, he thought, she would respond.

But suddenly Erin was fighting him, fighting for her life. The anger in his voice, the roughness of his touch, seemed to trigger memories, memories of Ralph's pawing hands, his verbal abuse, his physical abuse. The bitterness, the grief, the humiliation, all washed over her, inundating her, frightening her.

"No," she whispered, twisting and flailing him.

"Oh, yes," he muttered determinedly, "I've had enough arguments and refusals. It seems that you are a total coward. If it only affected you, it would be one thing. But it doesn't. It affects me, and I intend to fight for what I want out of life, and right now I want you, Erin."

"Oh, no!" she grated, the adrenaline pumping through her body, giving her the strength to break out of his grasp. "Not like this!" Tears filled her eyes and spilled down her cheeks. "Why is it," she demanded, her voice shaky with anger, with pain, "when a man can't get a woman to do what he wants, he resorts to physical force. Why is he so hell-bent on making her bend to his will? Never any consideration for her wishes or feelings!" The tears ran unchecked, and she held her hands up, warding him off, as she backed up. "Tell me, Devlin." Her defiance changed to a heart-stirring sob. "Tell me if you can?"

He shook his head, breathing raggedly and deeply. "I'm sorry, baby. I didn't mean to frighten you."

"Not just you," she snapped savagely, refusing to be

mollified this easily, with just a few words. "Ralph too. When he couldn't pull me down to his gutter-level, he began running around with other women. When he couldn't find his manhood in a bottle, he thought he could find it beating me into submission." She turned her back on him, dropping her head, the gesture completely undoing Devlin. "No, thank you, Mr. Douglas," she breathed wearily, her anger dissipating, "I've had enough of this kind of love to last me several lifetimes."

"Erin," he pleaded, his control about to break, "my God, how could you think for an instant I would hurt you? I admit I was going to try to break your resistance by making love to you, but no more." He took a step, but Erin, sensing his nearness, flung her head over her shoulder and glared at him. "I love you, Erin," he told her. "I love you too much to hurt you. Do you understand me?"

Erin moved again, putting more distance between them. When she stood at the dresser, she yanked a tissue from the dispenser, gingerly dabbing her cheeks and eyes, trying not to smear her makeup.

"Are you going to answer me?"

She held the tissue to her cheek, but her eyes were looking at his reflection in the mirror, and she couldn't have broken contact if she had wanted to. She saw the truth in his eyes, and she heard the love ringing in his voice.

She nodded. "I understand." He had to strain to hear the words. "I'm—I—" She stammered. "I told you that I'm still a coward." She smiled sheepishly. "It'll take me a little while to get over Ralph."

Devlin walked to where she stood and gently laid his hands on her shoulders. "I love you, Erin, and I'm sorry if I acted the part of the brute. Forgive me?" She nodded. "Do you remember last Thursday night?" he asked, his breath stirring the strands of hair that lay on her shoulder.

"You asked me to make love to you?" She nodded. "Well, I am, darling," he said with a vulnerability that tore into Erin's soul. "Whether you love me or not, whether you can love me or not." He turned her around in his arms.

"Thank you, Devlin," she whispered, her eyes again brimming with tears. "And I'll give you all of myself that I can."

CHAPTER SEVEN

The room was bathed in the soft light from the single bed lamp, and Erin, exhausted with her unsuccessful fight with insomnia, stood in the open terrace doors, dressed only in a nightgown. As she stared at the panoramic view of Houston at midnight, she briefly thought about her early meeting the next morning, but she didn't plan to go back to bed. Not even the brisk November night could persuade her differently.

Sleep not only evaded her, she reflected, but it was mocking her, denying her the privilege of escaping Devlin's haunting presence. He was still here with her, thrusting himself into her mind, burning his imprint indelibly into her memory. It was as if she had no memories that were not bound in one way or the other with him.

Sighing, she flexed her shoulders and reached up with one hand to cup the nape of her neck, her long fingers kneading the tense muscles. She would never forget these holidays; she would never forget the warmth and friendliness of Devlin's family. It would be so easy, she mused, so very easy to let go, to love them, to love him. *So*, she asked herself, *if that's the case, why don't you do it?*

Leaning against the doorjamb, she peered over her shoulder, glancing at the discarded black satin robe that lay on the bed. After Devlin had dropped her off and had left to take the girls home, she had showered and dressed, expecting him to return shortly. After all, he had promised to come back, she thought, her eyes unconsciously flitting over the low, contemporary-style dresser, lingering on her favorite bottle of perfume, remembering drops that had been secreted in sensually strategic places, the tantalizing fragrance constantly reminding her of the silence and the loneliness.

He had tenderly commanded, "Keep the light burning, darling," when he'd left to take the girls home, but his call a few hours later had released her from the loving injunction. "Sorry, baby," he had softly intoned, "I can't make it back. Evidently Mrs. Hooper isn't returning from her son's until tomorrow."

The day and the evening had been too beautiful to end like this, Erin mused sadly, but it wasn't anyone's fault really. Still, she hurt, and still, she was jealous. Jealous because Devlin couldn't be with her. Jealous because they couldn't be together. Sharing him with the girls would be no obstacle, Erin thought. But she didn't like this.

She smiled as she recalled the drive home from Seguin with the girls and Devlin. Quietly she chuckled when she remembered their big Saturday night out. The girls, reluctant for the holidays to end, squeezed every ounce of pleasure out of the weekend that they could, and she and Devlin had willingly complied. The girls' wishes were their commands.

After all the pizza they could eat and the cola they could drink, Devalind and Nanette had begged Devlin to take them to a movie. After Devlin agreed, the girls informed him that the next showing was at nine o'clock, but they quickly suggested with mischievously twinkling eyes, they could pass the time by shopping at the mall. Happily

Devlin and Erin had deferred once again to their demands.

Slowly they had meandered from one end of the gigantic mall to the other, moving from store to store, doing more window shopping than buying. Finally when they stopped outside a pet shop, oohing and aahing over the little puppies, an elderly couple joined them, watching the antics of the girls more than those of the animals.

"Your family is so lovely," the woman had said to Erin. "The older one looks like her father, but this one—" she touched Nanette on the crown of her head "—looks just like you."

"I do?" Nanette piped up, her interest completely diverted from the dogs.

Devlin, as astounded as Nanette, slowly turned and looked at both Erin and his daughter. He hadn't thought about it before, but they did look alike. Not that Erin resembled Nancy, he conceded, his eyes narrowing, darkening, focusing on Erin's flaming face. It was that classical bone structure, he decided. The blue eyes.

"Yes," he drawled slowly, nodding his head, surprised with the discovery, "Netty does look like her." He smiled broadly at the woman and draped his arm over Erin's shoulder, pulling her closer to him. "Most people claim that Lindy looks like me and Netty like her mother." His face tipped downward, and he smiled directly into Erin's face, their secret twinkling in his eyes.

"Such a lovely couple," the woman had said later to her husband as they walked away. "So delightful."

"And I agree wholeheartedly," Devlin whispered into Erin's ear. "I think you and I make a lovely couple. So delightful."

The girls giggled, and Nanette cocked her head to one side, mimicking the departing woman, "I think you do, too, MOTHER! So-o-o-o delightful!"

And the evening had continued with the same levity.

They had laughed over nothing and over everything before they left the Galleria to catch the nine o'clock showing of their movie. Erin wasn't sure what they saw; she didn't care. She had been lost in her moment with Devlin, and nothing else had mattered. She had basked in the magic of their being together, in the beauty of their togetherness.

Their togetherness had brought about an intimacy that had always been unknown to Erin. The joy of sharing had startled her, making her feel awkward and gauche. But the girls didn't seem to notice her reticence, and Devlin overlooked it. Happily Devalind and Nanette had supplied her with a running commentary of the movie as they plied her and Devlin with refreshments.

After a while the girls had settled down, engrossed in the story, and Erin and Devlin were left to their own devices. They fed each other popcorn from the same box and slurped Coke from the same glass. For dessert they licked the same ice cream cone. Afterwards they sat so close that their shoulders touched, and they held hands. Once or twice they had turned their faces toward each other at the same time, and Devlin had lightly tweaked Erin's nose with his lips. They whispered and laughed, oblivious to the glares and shushes of the people around them.

Without making love to her, he had loved her, totally and completely. He had made her feel very special and cared for. He had covered her with the protection of his love. And now she was hurt and deprived. She missed his attention; she missed his presence. She was so lonely she could hardly stand it. The quietness of the house had an unsettling quality, and the aloneness suffocated her. After a while she had shed her satin robe, tossing it on the end of the bed.

She had tried to sleep, but she couldn't. Thoughts of Devlin, though unbidden and resented, kept pushing themselves into the forefront of her mind. All she could think about was Devlin. He was in all her thoughts; he was her thoughts. It was hard for her to remember a time in her life when there was no Devlin Douglas. She wanted to be near him; she wanted to hear him laugh again; she wanted him to whisper love words in her ear again.

The night was long and lonely without him, and she couldn't see the beauty of the city lights for missing him. *Please, let him come back,* her soul supplicated. *Please, let him come to hold me, to love me through the loneliness of the dark night.*

How long she stood there, praying for Devlin's return, she didn't know, but it felt like an eternity. And when the doorbell shattered the silence, she knew that it was he. She wanted to move, but she couldn't. Her eyes darted from the satin robe to the nightgown she was wearing. And as the chimes continued to echo, breaking the sad silence, impatiently heralding Devlin's arrival, she quickly spun around.

Hurriedly she closed and locked the terrace doors, running across the room, a smile spanning the width of her face. She tugged on the satin robe, tying the sash around her waist. By this time Devlin was leaning heavily on the doorbell, and the continuous sound reverberated through the room. A soft chuckle slipped past Erin's smiling lips.

Devlin, tired of waiting, hunched his shoulders against the cool wind and pressed on the doorbell again. What was keeping her, he wondered, shuffling his feet on the large welcome mat. He expected her to be waiting. She had to know that it was him. He stepped back, his eyes scaling the front of the house. But no light of life flickered in the windows. Again he pressed the doorbell.

"Come on," he muttered softly. "Where are you, Erin?"

Surely she hadn't gone out after he called! She wouldn't have done that! Surely not! He jabbed the doorbell forcibly, venting his frustration on it. Once! Twice! Three times! Maybe she was a heavy sleeper. But even a heavy sleeper would be awake by now! He doubled up his fist and began to pound on the door.

Erin stopped to catch her breath and to still the erratic beating of her heart. She had to grin at Devlin's impatience as she called out, "Just a minute. I'm coming."

Dexterously she flipped the lock and unhooked the night latch with one hand, grasping the doorknob with the other, gently squeezing and pulling at the same time. Without waiting for her to open the door, Devlin shoved, sweeping into the room.

"What took you so long?" he demanded, his voice gruff with worry. "I thought something had happened to you."

"No," she murmured, again touched by his caring, "nothing happened."

He paused. "Were you asleep?"

"No," she answered in that same soft voice, locking the door, turning and leaning against it, "I wasn't sleeping." She smiled, the gesture so beautiful and sweet that it caressed Devlin's heart. "I was thinking about you, hoping you would come after all."

"But what took you so long?" he asked, shrugging out of his jacket, carelessly slinging it across the nearest chair.

"I had to put something on," she whispered, looking at the tousled black hair that gleamed blue in the soft light that filtered from her bedroom. She looked at the form-fitting jeans that clearly outlined the muscles in his thighs. She looked at the green silk shirt that was taut across the sinewy chest. But she saw far more than that. She saw beyond the craggy exterior to the man beneath all the calloused surface. She saw the tenderness and the gentleness; she saw love with no limit.

"The robe's beautiful," he countered softly, his eyes hotly brushing over the sweep of her breasts, the fitted waistline, the flowing lines of the shiny material over her hips. "And so are you." Again he took in the full sweep of the black satin robe before he looked at her face. The raven-black eyes were softly feathered with glints of sparkling happiness as he murmured, "But putting it on was such a waste of energy."

"I didn't think so." The words butterflied across the distance. "I thought you wanted to undress me."

"I do, my darling." His quiet chuckle was deep and soothed her like the touch of a thick, soft, and sweet-smelling towel after a hot bath. "I want to be the only man who's undressing you, the only man in your life."

"You are," she promised him.

"And maybe someday," he continued, "I'll be the only man in your heart, the only one to have entered there."

The aura of serene joy that permeated Erin's entire being, radiating her face, didn't diminish, but the glow in her eyes became shadowed. "Perhaps," was her soft, tentative reply. They stared at each other for a few seconds in the sensually charged room, Erin finally breaking the silence. "Mrs. Hooper made it back after all?"

"No."

"Where are the girls then?"

"At Holley's."

"Who's Holley?"

"Their Grandmother Holloway." He couldn't suppress the grin.

"You mean—"

"I mean," he gently mocked. "I drove them over to her house."

"And she doesn't mind?"

"Well," Devlin drawled, not bothering to hide the amusement that lurked in those black eyes, "I didn't exactly tell Holley that I was leaving the girls with her so I could spend the night with you."

"What did you tell her?" Erin asked, her lips twitching with delight.

"Nothing really," Devlin retorted. "I just sorta let nature take its course."

Erin's brows rose. "With absolutely no help from you?"

He grinned and shrugged. "Well, now, maybe just a little bit of help. When the girls called to let her know that we were home, she invited them to come out tomorrow."

"And you sorta suggested that they go spend the night?" Erin quizzed.

"Sorta," he parried gently. "And I promised Holley that I'd bring you with me when I came to get the girls."

"I'm—" Erin's face was blank with surprise. "You want me to go to your mother-in-law's?"

"For lunch, no less," Devlin chuckled. "I can hardly wait to introduce you to her."

Erin shook her head. "Too much is happening too quickly Devlin. Can you imagine how she'll feel about meeting me?"

He nodded, a momentary sadness clouding his eyes and face. "She wants to meet you, Erin. She's interested in the girls and me." He could still see the uncertainty in Erin's eyes, the question on her face. "Holley loved Nancy, but she can't bring her back, Erin. And just because I was married to her daughter at one time, Holley won't stand in the way of my happiness or the girls' happiness. You'll soon learn that Holley is very much a part of our lives. I want Lindy and Netty to know and to love both sets of grandparents. Even more, I want them to have a close relationship to Holley. They're all she has left of Nancy besides her memories." He smiled slowly. "Any more questions."

"Not for the time being," she murmured, gazing into his face, marveling at his strength, thankful for his softness. She had never felt the warm cloak of love before, and she was almost frightened to reach out and take what Devlin offered, but she would. "I think this is the time for us."

Devlin threw back his head and laughed in relief, the resonant tones rumbling from the muscular chest cavity, gently massaging Erin's sensitized nerve endings, easing that ache in her heart, causing a deeper ache in her soul. In long strides he crossed the floor, but Erin moved before he reached her. She turned, not from his embrace but to guide him—and she walked toward the pie-shaped gleam of light that fanned from her bedroom. Devlin hesitated; then she heard his footsteps as they quietly squished on the thick carpet. He was following her.

She was nervous, but she didn't show it. Steadily she moved across the terra-cotta-colored carpet, through the bedroom door, past the bed, to stand in front of the terrace doors. Devlin, however, stopped at the foot of the bed, carefully surveying the large room that reflected yet another facet of Erin's personality, revealing her sweet essence.

Her furniture was contemporary in style, the accent pieces in rattan. The colors were bold and hot, most unusual, he decided, his eyes fluttering to the paintings that hung on either side of the bed.

"Sunrises or sunsets?" he asked, then added, "Or both?"

"Sunrise on the left and sunset on the right," she murmured softly, still not turning, not looking at him.

"I've never seen these colors together," he commented, his eyes slowing trailing from the peach-colored drapes and bedspread, to the throw pillows in lavender, rose, and magenta.

"You've seen them," she returned dryly in an undertone. "You've just never noticed them." She pointed to one of the paintings. "See the sunrise or the sunset, Devlin. Really look at it."

Devlin moved closer to the painting, stopping directly in front of it, studying it. "I don't guess I've ever really seen a sunset," he observed quietly. "Never really seen one." He looked at all the colors that radiated from the sinking golden orb. "Water color?"

"Yes," she replied, waiting tensely, wondering if he'd notice.

"It's beautiful, Erin. So delicate. So real. It speaks to me." His eyes swept over the painting. "Who painted—" Just as the "it" slipped past his lips, he saw the signature in the bottom left corner. "You painted this!"

Erin smiled, hugging herself, happy with the pride she heard in his exclamation. "Yes."

"How about the other one?"

"My art instructor did that one for me."

"A woman of many talents," he praised.

Erin chuckled, thinking back to her childhood, remembering her favorite teacher. "Sister Anna Maria used to accuse me of being a jack of all trades and master of none. She stayed exasperated with me because I'd throw something aside once I'd learned that I could do it and do it well."

Devlin laughed with her, momentarily seeing her with all her barriers down. And then the time for reminiscing was over; the time for light conversation to cease. Softly he called. "Erin."

Erin said nothing. She could no more obey the sensual command than she could look into Devlin's face. She turned instead, running her fingers up and down the drape.

"What's wrong?" Devlin asked, never raising his voice, trying desperately to hide his anxiety.

"Nothing," she whispered, wondering what Devlin would think of her after they had made love. Wondering if she would be a disappointment to him. Wondering if he would be a disappointment to her. Dare she risk it! Dare she put herself in such a position again! Could she withstand another hurt?

"Something's wrong, baby," he asserted, "or you

wouldn't have withdrawn so quickly. You seemed happy enough a minute ago, and you acted like you wanted me to stay." He waited, but she made no reply. "Are you having second thoughts, Erin? Do you want to change your mind?" She shook her head, and he sighed. "Do you want me to stay?"

Erin ran her tongue over her parched lips, letting her faint yes drift across the room. Still, she didn't turn around. Still, she felt too vulnerable.

"Turn around and look at me then."

She heard the command spoken softly; she heard the plea that braced it. Slowly she turned her head, but she didn't move otherwise. She couldn't. Her feet felt as if they were weighted with lead; they were too heavy for her to move. Her wanting Devlin to stay the night, her having acknowledged that she wanted him to stay made her choice no easier. She was out of her depth emotionally, and she was afraid. She was too scared to move.

Devlin saw her glance around, and he saw the expression on her countenance change as she pondered the situation. He wondered what she was thinking, and erroneously believed that she was about to change her mind. As for himself, he'd had enough of these childish games, but he was intelligent enough to recognize that Erin, for all her maturity, was a shy, sensitive woman. He couldn't force her. This he knew. He could only love her into submission. Biting back any barbed comments, he held his hand out.

"Come here, darling."

The injunction, cloaked in velvet, was her undoing. She turned completely, trailing her tongue sensuously over her full lips. "I'll come to you," she compromised, "if you'll come to me at the same time." Anxiously she looked into the raven-colored eyes.

"I'll come," he promised, his firm lips slowly beginning to curve into that smile that radiated from the eyes to the lips, settling into the grooves at the corners of his mouth. His hand still extended, he moved.

And then she was moving toward him, and it was as if she were floating instead of walking. Intoxicated by his presence and his nearness, she never took her eyes from his face. Nothing was real but her and Devlin. Then he lifted his hands, and, spellbound, she watched him as he began to undress.

His hand touched the center top of his shirt, and steadily his fingers worked on the buttons. Erin's eyes greedily feasted on the powerful masculinity that was revealed when the soft green material parted. She inhaled deeply when she saw the dark mat of hair that spread from the chest downward, veeing into the waistband of his jeans. Her eyes swept over his physique, burning him with her visual touch, setting him on fire with the passion that simmered in her being.

They were together, his arms around her, her arms around him. Even in the dim light, however, Erin could feel the warmth of his glance. She could see the hunger in his eyes. Both could feel the desire that flowed between them; both could see and feel the anticipation that welled in the other, that overflowed, spilling over both of them.

"Don't be frightened," Devlin soothed her, remembering her soft confessions on several other occasions, troubled by her hesitancy because he didn't understand the reason for it. "I'll never do anything to hurt you." His lips moved gently over the tender curve of her ear, and his nostrils filled with that delicate, illusive fragrance that was Erin.

"I'm not afraid anymore," she whispered, her lips moving against the moist warmth of his bronze collarbone, her hands touching the smooth flesh of his stomach, traveling under his arms to his back. "I—I see you, Devlin."

He tensed. He waited. "You see me?" The words were faint.

"Yes," she confessed on a joyful sigh, "I can see you." Her breath whispered over his skin, causing him to tingle from head to toe with burning desire. Her confession caressed his heart, filling his soul with the exultant melody of love.

"I knew it," he laughed, lifting her in his arms, swinging her around. "I knew it could be like this."

Erin laughed with him, holding on as he spun her around, gasping her happiness when he stopped and held her close to him.

"Oh, God, Erin, you're so good for me." And his mouth sought hers.

Before he could kiss her, however, she said, "You're good for me too. I—I just hope I'm good in—in—"

Devlin understood and placed a finger across her mouth, quieting her. "You will be, sweet darling. You will be."

"I—I haven't had much experience." Her voice shook with her confession.

"This isn't a job, sweetheart," he returned with soft amusement. "No experience is necessary."

Erin laughed with him, her fingers splaying against his chest, rubbing through the thick mat of hair. "As old as I am," she continued, losing her inhibitions, "I don't know where to begin."

"I'm a willing teacher," he supplied.

"Then teach me, Devlin," she implored him from the bottom of her heart. "Teach me to love you."

Hoarsely he grated against her ear, his arms tightening into bands of steel around her body. "You're doing great, sweetheart. Just great." A low husky whisper brushed against the tendrils of hair that covered her ear. "Both of us have a lot of learning to do, and we'll learn together. We'll guide each other."

She nodded, mesmerized by the sonorous intonations, by his virility, and his nearness. His fingers fastened on the sash of her robe, stopping just long enough to untie it. Then he pushed the soft material off her shoulders, letting it swish to the floor, to lie in a shiny pool around her feet. He looked at the black satin gown she wore, wondering at the beauty it yet concealed, which was yet to be revealed to his hungering eyes.

"I'm glad you wanted me to stay." His words were caressing and soft, so faint Erin could hardly hear them.

"I had no choice," she murmured, not wanting to break the sweetness of the moment. How long had she dreamed of the time when she would have a man like Devlin coming to her! How often had she wanted a man like him to love her! How long had she hungered for someone to touch her? To move her? "Absolutely no choice," she sighed.

"Nor did I." The admission came as no surprise to either one of them. "From the first minute I set eyes on you, Erin, I knew you were going to play an important role in my life. I knew it was in the cards for you and me to love each other."

He pulled back and looked at her, at the gown, the satin so smooth, so shining, the material so clinging, accenting the gentle swell of her breasts, the flatness of her stomach, the rounded curve of her hips. Two small black straps tormentingly accented the creamy whiteness of her shoulders, and the black lace that covered the fullness of her breasts hinted at the pearly beauty that it hid.

"I think you've finally convinced me," she said, eagerly embracing him, her arms sliding up and down his back, her hands running the full length of his spine.

"It's about time," he murmured, his hands, playing Follow the Leader with hers, doing the same, whispering across her back, not in comfort, but in blatant, lustful arousal, whetting the ardor between them.

"Yes," she admitted softly, "it is." She slipped her hands under his shirt, sliding it off his shoulders, her fingers grasping the muscled flesh, kneading it, tantalizing him with her sweet touch, with her hunger. Her mouth, moving slowly, traveled the entire span of his chest, her lips nipping, biting, caressing, until they finally circled one of the brown nipples that nestled in the furry mat of hair. As her lips pouted, her tongue swirled around, teasing him, the wet tip tormentingly brushing against the distended masculine peak.

"Erin," he gasped lovingly, "I can't remember when I've wanted to make love as much as I want to make love to you now. For so long it's been nothing more than sex."

He nuzzled her face, loving the softness, loving the feel of her warm, moist skin, loving her touch. Of all the women he'd been with during the past few years, none had totally satisfied him. True, his sexual desires had been appeased, but that deep, nagging hunger for a wife or a lover in a complete sense had never been abated since Nancy's death. And now, he thought, again whiffing that erotic perfume, this woman promised to be that fulfillment. She would be the only person capable of assuaging his burning desires, the only one who could satisfy his needs.

Erin cuddled closer to him, their bodies, their emotions, attuned. Without knowing, she understood all his thoughts, she sensed all his feelings. "It took you so long," she whispered. "I didn't think you'd be over tonight."

"I came as soon as I could," he told her. "I didn't want to call you in front of the girls, and I didn't dare call from Holley's." They both laughed together. "When Holley suggested that the girls come over to spend the day tomorrow, I had to insist on tonight as well. I had to be with you, little angel." His mouth moved against her face, her lips, her cheeks, her ears.

Although his entire body ached for her, ached for release, he was in no hurry. He had the rest of his life to love her, and he fully intended to love her the rest of his life.

She moved him as no one, including Nancy, had moved him. She had shaken him to the very core of his being, making him aware of a void in his life. Everything she did—her laughter, her anger, her fears, her doubts—touched him. He desired to soothe her, to taste her goodness, to share her love, to merge with her softness and her femininity.

As his mouth brushed along her cheek, he again inhaled the sweetness of her perfume, her lotion, her soap, herself, and a small sound of satisfaction gurgled from the back of his throat. Then his tongue tipped around the tender outer curve of her ear, sending a shiver of anticipation and pleasure through her.

"Why—why have we waited so long?" she asked tremulously, quaking in his arms.

"It wasn't we, darling. It was you."

She laughed with him, dizzy with excitement, inebriated with ecstasy. She lifted her hand and cupped his face, her lips tentatively beginning their exploration of his face. Surrendering to her ministrations of love, he allowed her lips to travel randomly over his beard-stubbled cheeks, to feather light kisses over his lips and chin. He shivered when her tongue burrowed in the sensitive hollow at the base of his neck.

With a growl of pleasure he swooped her into his arms and carried her to the bed, gently laying her down, lying down beside her. "I'm so glad that we're finally together," he sighed, caressing her shoulders, trailing kisses down the line of the black strap of the gown and across the creamy smoothness of her breasts. His lips lingered, teasing, feathering warm nibbles, causing Erin to shiver. "You're mine," he murmured, using love talk that was more affective then literal. "All mine." His lips continued to explore, moving over the material that covered her nipples, to the midriff, blowing his hot breath through the satin to her skin. "You don't—" He chanted between caresses. "You can't belong to anyone else." His hands continued to massage her shoulders and she began to move her body closer to him, burrowing into his strength. As he quietly spoke to her, his mouth at her ear, his fingers swirled lower and lower, moving from the base of her neck, sliding beneath the delicate lace at the bodice of her nightgown, stimulating and tensing the poised nerve endings in her breasts.

"Devlin," she gasped in a tiny voice, her hand covering his. "I—you're—"

She couldn't complete her sentence any more than she could stop Devlin. She didn't know what she was trying to say; she couldn't think. But all the while that she wrestled with these chaotic emotions, her body spoke for itself. It moved sensuously against the lean, hard length of the man. And the man moved with her, against her, pressing the hardness of his body closer and closer, acquainting her with his throbbing desire, his voice softly cooing love.

When she could stand no more, she turned over, and his hands greedily cupped both her breasts, brushing over the sensitive skin of her midriff. She was dizzy with breathless delight and sucked in her stomach as she gasped, convulsive ripples shuddering through her frame. His fingers crooked under the straps of the gown, and Erin lifted herself, helping him as he slipped the black satin below her waist.

When his fingers splayed across her stomach, the tips touched the frothy lace of her bikini panties. He chuckled softly, his lips gently kissing from her shoulders, to her breasts, to her flat stomach, not stopping until they reached the panty line. "Do you always sleep in your panties?" he murmured, his warm breath fanning the silky texture of her skin.

"No," Erin breathed, her fingers tangling in the thick, black waves of his hair. "Maybe—" she could hardly talk "—my last defense against you." She closed her eyes in wondrous rapture as she continued to move her body in seductive rhythm to his demanding caresses.

"Nothing could keep me from you," he muttered thickly, his body pounding with his desire, the hotness flowing from his body to hers, inflaming her with the fiery blaze of his longings. His fingers spread, slid under the lace, and stiffened, stretching the elastic, pushing another unwanted garment down her legs, dropping it over the edge of the bed.

Erin curved her body, a beautiful graceful movement, and she reached for Devlin. Once again she began to make love to him, adding fuel to the already blazing fire of passion. She pressed her naked upper body to him, her arms urgently winding around his back and his neck. Frantically, almost with desperation, her lips sought his, finding them, tasting them, eating their honeyed sweetness.

Never in her life, never had she been this caught up in the throes of passion. Never had she allowed another human, another man, access to her intimate self as she was allowing Devlin. As easily as he had stripped her clothes from her body tonight, she shed her years of coldness, disdain, and indifference. She lay beside Devlin physically and emotionally baring herself.

Her mouth moved over Devlin's again and again, her lips swollen and red. Still they craved more and more of Devlin. Her tongue, a flaming arrow of love, pierced through the chiseled lips, burning the deepness with her penetrating assault, alerting him to her desperate needs. She left no territory unexplored, eagerly discovering and claiming as hers every inch of that musky terrain.

Devlin, finally breaking the kiss, gulping in air, buried his face in the silken waves that tangled over her shoulders. "Take it easy, sweetheart," he rejoined hoarsely, pulling his head back. He breathed in and out a few times, lifting his hands to cup her face, his lips softly brushing hers. A faint triumphant smile glowed in the depth of those ebony eyes. "I don't want to rush things." He lowered his face, his lips traveling down her neck as she arched her face backward, sounds of pleasure gurgling from her throat.

"I want it slow and easy, a lingering pleasure. I want to hold back as long as I can." He spoke and he kissed her at the same time, his mouth working against the corners of hers, his tongue teasing them open. "I've waited a long time for a woman like you, Erin, and I don't want to hurry it up."

"Oh, Devlin," she cried incoherently, "I've never felt like this before." She looked at him through tear-spiked lashes, her confession prayer soft and reverent. "I don't want to wait." She added on a much fainter note, "I don't know if I can or not."

He laughed exultantly, drunk with happiness. "Oh, angel, you're so wonderful." His voice was deep and vibrant. "You're so wonderful to hold, to taste, to feel." His lips moved knowingly over her face, down her neck, pausing at that small cavity that rested just above her collarbone, down the rounded swell of her breasts. Breathing warmly against her creamy skin, he commanded softly, "Touch me, darling. Touch me all over. Set me on fire like I'm setting you on fire. Love me." His hands caught hers, placing them on the waistband of his jeans. His lips wandered over her spicy-scented skin, and he murmured hotly, "Undress me, sweetheart. Finish undressing me."

Erin heard the sweet command, and she obeyed. Sitting up, she leaned down, taking off first his shoes and his socks. Next her hands touched the belt buckle. Then he was helping her, jeans and briefs falling into a discarded heap on the floor. Nothing was between them now. They looked at each other a long time before Erin's arms circled his body, her hands drawing his heavy, muscle-corded body over hers, the crushing pressure a sweet torment that elicited a soft moan of pleasure from her.

"Not so quick," he again reprimanded in a gravelly undertone, his voice thick with passion. He pulled back to look into her love-glazed eyes. "Let's savor this moment." He chuckled, reaching up with one finger to trace the outline of her eyebrows, her cheekbones, her nose. "Both of us can afford to prolong the pleasure." When her lips trembled under the soft tip of his finger and when she shook her head, he caught her in his arms, crushing her to his steely chest. "It's been a long time," he explained, "since I've wanted to go slow with a woman, since I've really wanted to make love. Let me be gentle with you. Let me take my time. Let me enjoy it with you. Please."

She nodded her head against his shoulder, her face feeling the wiry black curls that matted the bronze sheen of his body. She squeezed her eyes shut, savoring the beauty of the moment, basking in love for the first time in her life. She tasted its sweetness and its goodness. She drank its coolness and its fire. But try as she may, her tears of joy wouldn't be dammed, and they poured from her deepest self, purging her from an old festering wound.

She hadn't cried, really cried, since Jeremy. She hadn't cried for Ralph or for what they could have had. She couldn't cry for the baby that she'd lost. She had wanted to. The pain had been excruciating, and she had wanted to cry, but she couldn't. Her hurt was too deep and too grievous. Her soul had ceased to cry. It was as if she herself had died with the child. Now she cried.

Devlin felt the tears, and he pushed her away. "Erin—" he rolled away slightly, looking down at her "—why are you crying?"

Perplexity, like dark storm clouds, whirled in his eyes. He couldn't understand this woman. He could truthfully say she was an enigma to him. Might always be. Would she always be so near to him yet so far away? Would she never trust him?

She didn't answer. She just dropped her head, nestling against his chest, snuggling up to him, drawing comfort from his strength.

"Erin—" His hand touched her chin, and he lifted her face. "Look at me." She kept her eyes closed, but she made no attempt to wipe the tears from her cheeks. "Open your eyes." The command was gentle and soft.

She shook her head. She didn't think she could bear to look at him. She had felt vulnerable the night she had confided in him. She had felt vulnerable when they walked into the bedroom earlier. But at this moment with his seeing the liquid of her soul running down her cheeks, she was naked—totally naked.

"Please, Erin, open your eyes and look at me."

The cajoling tones were soothing; they were sweet. His tongue carefully followed the trail of tears, wiping them away, sweeping against the fiery heat of her cheeks, sending shivers of pleasure through her body and her soul. Finally, when she was breathing deeply and erratically, she lifted her glistening lashes and gazed into his face. The beauty she saw there, the kindness, the gentleness, knocked the breath out of her, and she was suspended somewhere. His eyes were soft and warm; they were passionate and loving. They promised.

"You lied to me," he gently surmised, the raven-black eyes searching the blue ones that were sparkling with unshed tears. "There have been no men in your life since Ralph." He looked beyond her face and her eyes; he looked into her soul, seeking the truth. "It's been a long time for you, hasn't it, honey?" Erin sobbed deeply, swallowing her tears. "It's been a long time since you've made love, hasn't it?"

Erin nodded. "I—" She began, only to break off again,

overcome with an emotion she'd never felt before. "I've—I've never made love, Devlin. I told you that before."

"I'm going to give you a taste of love that you'll never forget. I'm going to move you out of that ivory tower. From tonight on you'll know that you're capable of feeling again, darling."

He promised himself at that very instance that he would destroy all Erin's haunting memories. He would free her. And when she was free, she could love again. She could make the decision to love. Perhaps the decision to love him.

Then all coherent talk turned into fevered endearments of love, the sounds lost in the sweetness of the moment. Arms entwined, legs entwined, mouths pressed together, finding all the beautiful and pleasant paths of delight. Devlin, content for the time being, loved Erin, guiding her to that ecstatic fulfillment that she'd never experienced before, concentrating on her joy.

Later he would hold her in the darkness and listen as she confessed the anguish of her soul. He would listen as she told him all about Jeremy, all about Ralph, all about her baby. And he would protect her with all his strength, harboring her in the safety of his love.

CHAPTER EIGHT

"Like it?" Devlin asked, parking the car in front of the hotel on the outskirts of Monterrey.

"Umm-hmm," Erin breathed, her eyes sweeping over the white stucco building with its red-tiled roof. Rolling down her window, she inhaled the fragrance of the brightly colored flowers that bloomed profusely under the canopy of verdant trees that surrounded and sheltered the hotel. "As many times as I've been to Mexico, I've never been here," she marveled, looking around, drinking in the wondrous beauty. "It's so peaceful and quiet. So lovely."

Devlin, looking at her rather than the scenery, smiled his agreement. The ebony eyes, hidden by sunglasses, slowly and lovingly examined the woman sitting beside him—the black slacks; the blouse with a swirling design in black, red, and white; the golden-blond hair hanging in gentle waves over her shoulders.

"Very lovely," he murmured seductively, pulling his sunglasses off, laying them on the dash.

His tone alerted Erin to the intimacy of his thoughts, and she swiveled her head, slanting her eyes, grinning at him. "I think, perhaps, Mr. Douglas, that you and I are on two different wave lengths."

He shook his head. "You'd like to think that maybe, but we're not. I've been trying to tell you for the past five months we're on the very same wave length."

Looking deeply into those dark eyes, Erin drew her breath in, short and shallow, and her heart fluttered wildly. When she was with him, she became prey to that chemistry that was between them. And as always, despite her rationality, it grew out of control. This sexuality was something tangible between them and while it fascinated her and totally captivated her, it also frightened her.

Yet she couldn't deny that it existed. Both of them knew it; both of them felt it; and both of them succumbed to it. But, as of now, she hadn't identified her feelings for him as love. She could freely and readily admit that she needed and wanted Devlin in her life. She had to have him. But, still . . . She and Devlin weren't looking for the same thing in a relationship.

Losing herself in the swirling eddy of love in his eyes, she averted her head. "How—how did you find this place?" She changed the subject deliberately, wanting to avoid the intimacy that Devlin had been seeking ever since they'd left Houston hours ago.

Sighing his exasperation and irritation, Devlin opened his door and got out of the car, walking around the hood. As he opened her door for her, he replied, "I found this little place several years ago when I first started working with Delgado."

"Does he live close by?" Erin asked curiously as she swung her legs out and stood up.

"He has a country place higher in the mountains," he returned absently. "This became my retreat. Every time I've needed a breath of fresh air or time to myself, I've come up here."

Erin pulled the strap of her purse over her shoulder, and

she peeked at Devlin, again surprised that this man who awed so many and totally dwarfed his competitors could be such a dreamy romantic. Five months ago she wouldn't have believed it. Now she smiled, almost feeling a protectiveness for this lovable, gentle giant.

"Just your retreat?" she asked, giving emphasis to her words.

"My retreat," he answered, grinning into her face, sparks of devilment glinting in his eyes. "Why?" He didn't have to ask, but he did. He wanted Erin to verbalize her love for him, but if she couldn't do that yet, he, at least, wanted her to confess her jealousy.

She shrugged. "Just wondered." Was he speaking rhetorically, she asked herself. Does he really mean his retreat? For all she knew, he could make a habit of bringing the current woman in his life to this secluded paradise. Was this weekend just one of many to him, or was this as special for him as it was for her? When she lifted her thick lashes and stared into his face, she didn't bother to mask her questions.

Devlin suppressed another sigh, but his jaws flexed with his displeasure. Would Erin never trust him, he wondered. All he said, however, was, "I've never brought anyone else up here with me."

"No one?" she softly questioned, adding, "Not even Nancy or the girls?"

He shook his head. "No one, darling." He caught her in his arms, hugging her closely to him. "You're the first one to come with me. This will be our weekend." One hand cupped her chin, and he lifted her face, lowering his lips, gently touching hers, slowly moving his face from side to side, tormenting and tantalizing her, sampling the honeyed sweetness of her lips without eating of their succulence. "Happy birthday, darling."

Erin giggled, looping her arms around his neck, pulling his head down, pressing her lips solidly against his, taking the initiative. She wasn't about to let him tease her any longer. Softly, beautifully, her full red lips pouted and parted, her tongue wisping over his mouth, darting back and forth across the indentation where his lips met, trying to part them.

"Don't think you're going to hold out on me," she murmured. "You're not."

Enjoying the playful sexual antics, Devlin didn't open his mouth. His hands, however, joined in the love motions, and his fingers trailed hotly down her spine, closing around her waist. When her lips feathered his cheeks and temples, he whispered, "Maybe I will," but all the while he gathered her close to him.

Not accepting his gentle banter as an answer, Erin listened, rather, to his body and continued her assault, her hands dropping from his neck to his chest to his waist. She pulled his sweater up, and her fingers began to blatantly explore his rib cage, his chest, his back. Her hands roamed up and down his spine, finally letting her fingers move against his warm flesh, letting them move below his belt line.

"Give up?" she asked, touching her lips to his, her tongue nipping the nectar of her love on his lips, her fingers teasing the sensitive skin of his lower back, her hips pressed against his.

Devlin allowed himself the luxury of a small self-satisfied chuckle and opened his mouth, welcoming the thrusting invasion of Erin's tongue. He invited the fullness of her caress, his tongue touching and greeting hers. The kiss deepened, with Erin exploring all the wondrous delights of Devlin's mouth, searching for more, thirsty and hungry for all of him.

When she finally pulled away from him, her blue eyes were sparkling with life, warm with desire and passion. "By the way," she told him, "this isn't my birthday."

He grinned, his wandering hands slipping down to cup

the fullness of her buttocks. "Let's just pretend that it is. It'll give us something to celebrate."

"We celebrate every time we go out," she mocked him gently. "It's always an anniversary of something."

"A continuous celebration of love," he told her, seriousness darkening the ebony eyes even more and lowering that deep, mellow voice.

The evening continued on the same light-hearted note. They unpacked their luggage, bathed, and changed clothes. They ate their dinner in the hotel restaurant and spent the evening walking around the huge courtyard, finally sitting down on the wooden platform that extended over a small pool that was fed by a waterfall. For a long time they sat in silence, looking at the distant lights of Monterrey at the bottom of the mountain.

After a while Devlin stood and walked to the edge of the platform, leaning over to pick up some pebbles, straightening to throw them into the pool. Because the early spring evening was brisk, Erin pulled her sweater around her and looked at Devlin. Hungrily her eyes wandered over his frame, never tiring of his rugged good looks. Tonight his masculinity was enhanced by the slate gray turtleneck sweater, the lighter gray jacket, and the black slacks that he wore.

Aware of her scrutiny, Devlin turned his face, and the wind lightly tousled the thick mass of black hair that was parted on one side and brushed from his face. Those full lips quirked into a partial smile as he felt the touch of her blue eyes. The grooves at the corners of his mouth deepened, and Erin visually caressed them too.

She felt a growing need in the lower part of her body, the heat effusing throughout her entire being, boiling through her veins, threatening to erupt at any moment. Again she felt that invisible pull, that magnetism between them. She felt as if something were coercing her to want him, to desire him. No part of her was left untouched by this primitive urge.

Devlin held his hand out, and Erin, trancelike, rose, moved, and placed her hand in his. "Are you bored?" Concern thickened his voice.

"No," she whispered, pulling her hand from his grasp, lifting it, pushing a wisp of hair from her face. "I'm enjoying our being here."

"I'm glad." He stopped the movement of her hand, closing his around hers, bringing it down, placing it flat against his chest. Then he held her close, resting his chin on the mass of silken hair.

Wondering about his quietness and his withdrawal, afraid to ask why, Erin said, "I'm glad you brought me."

He hugged her tighter, and she rested her cheek on his chest. "Are you?" She felt his chest move as he spoke, and she gently nodded her head. "Have you thought about my question?"

The abrupt change in the conversation momentarily disconcerted Erin, but she should have known that the topic would eventually come up. She tensed, but she didn't push out of his arms. Rather, she snuggled closer, inhaling that familiar scent of his aftershave. She liked the softness of the sweater yarn; she liked the masculine scent; she liked the strength of the man underneath. She shoved her hands up under the sweater, pressing her palms to his flesh.

"Yes," she replied quietly, feeling him shiver from her ministrations of love, "I've thought about it." She said no more.

"And?" he queried softly, curiously.

Now she pushed herself out of his arms, carefully patting his sweater into place. She turned her back to him and walked away. Her voice was low but steady. "I'm not ready for a permanent relationship." How final it sounded, even to her. How cold.

Erin felt him as he walked up to her. She felt his hand feather lightly along the nape of her neck, beneath her hair, and the movement sent a delicious shimmer down her spine. She knew that his face was close to hers, but she didn't turn. Expectancy permeated downward into every muscle of her body and liquid fire flamed through her veins as her senses concentrated on the slow, deliberate motions of his fingers against her collarbone, against her neck.

"Why, Erin?" He never stopped touching her. Each movement was designed to torment, to make her aware of him and of his effect on her. He refused to let her evade his question; he refused to let her ignore it. He was determined that she would give him an answer. And the answer would be given tonight.

She shrugged and murmured, "I'm just not ready."

"Not good enough," he snapped.

Erin lifted her hand to her hair. "I don't like it when you use that tone of voice with me," she protested. "And I don't like it when you sound so dictatorial and possessive." She was angry, but not with him. She was angry with herself because she was afraid to love him. Afraid to make promises to him.

"I wish you felt the same way about me," he grated, recognizing his actions stemmed from his desperation. His love demanded more than she had been willing to give up to now. He needed all of her, and he wanted her to need him the same way. Yet she continued to plead for more time. And even now, with his knowing that she loved him, he also knew that she wouldn't admit that their attraction was more than chemistry.

"You promised that we'd take it one day at a time," she reminded him. "I would lead and you would follow."

"But the days have turned into months, and the months are about to turn into half a year. There's got to be a point where we stop playing Follow the Leader. A place where we walk side by side in some sort of permanent relationship."

He didn't attempt to hide his irritation. He was tired of just spending the night with her here and there, always one of them having to leave, not sure when they'd see each other again. He didn't like the vulnerability of loving without being loved in return. And he had the feeling that Erin would never admit her love for him.

"I love you, Erin, but I must have more than a bed partner. I want a partner for life." When she didn't answer, he caught both her shoulders with his hands, and he turned her around. "Can't you say something?"

"Nothing more than what I've already said."

"Dear, God," he muttered hoarsely, "why do I have to love you so much? It's tearing me apart, Erin."

His lips took hers gently, slowly, and Erin had no thoughts to deny him or herself. His hand slipped around her waist, and her lips parted against his increased dominance. Willingly she yielded herself to the heated fervor of his embrace, to the moist warmth of his mouth on hers. Her hand traveled up the familiar path from his chest to his shoulder, her fingers gripping into the muscled flesh, clinging while the other hand moved from his waist to the hard muscles of his back.

Devlin sensed her total response, and as usual it drove him over the brink of sanity. His grip on her waist tightened, and his kiss became more demanding. Although he was lost in a beautiful void, reality spinning away from him, he was unconsciously making Erin respond once again to the feelings that fused them together in oneness.

Pulling her mouth from his, Erin tucked her head against his chest, breathing deeply. "I was afraid that you'd get hurt," she told him. "I was afraid that you would ask too much and when I couldn't give it, you'd be hurt."

He lifted her chin with his hand, and his lips touched

hers again, persuading her, softly whispering over hers. "Why can't you give it to me, Erin?" Erin tried to twist out of his arms, but he held her fast. "I can't believe that you don't love me when you respond to me like you do. I just can't believe it." He pulled back and looked at her. "It's more a matter of your not wanting to do it than your not being able to."

Erin opened her mouth, and she attempted to speak, but no words would come. She and Devlin had been over this so many times. Discussion after discussion. Now the discussions were turning into arguments. And the arguments were increasing. She admitted that he created a world of ecstasy for her, and when she was with him, she had no thoughts but his thoughts, no wishes but his. She was totally captivated by the sensual magic only he could create for her.

Yet she struggled; she wrestled with her emotions. She had thought through her answer many times. She knew what she wanted for herself. She couldn't give in to the pleasure of the moment. She couldn't lose control of her destiny now.

Yet, as if he understood her need for space, his hands came to her shoulders, and he pushed her away. He moved back ever so slightly. "Why can't you make a commitment, Erin?"

She looked up at him, and in the soft light that filtered from the hotel, Devlin saw her face. The shadows, however, obscured the pain and grief that still lingered in their depths. When she spoke, her tone dropped in timbre.

"A relationship requires too much. It requires a special kind of commitment, the kind I can't afford to give right now." Her voice never wavered, and she looked directly into his face.

"Why not, I'm asking."

"I—" She paused. "I have other priorities in my life at present."

"Lindsay Machinery being numero uno!"

She nodded her head. "Yes, I've worked hard to salvage the company to make it what it is today." She didn't have to tell him how she'd worked to expand it, the hours, the energy, the money, the worry that she'd poured into it. He knew.

"You could still have your career and marriage too."

She shook her head. "I don't want marriage, Devlin." Her voice lowered another octave. "I keep telling you that. I don't want an emotional involvement." She jammed her hands into the pockets of her sweater and hunched her shoulders.

As she moved away from him, Devlin's hands dropped. "Involvements," he repeated dryly, running his finger idly over the railing of the platform. "I take it that you're referring to me and the girls."

"On a permanent basis—" she began "—on the basis that you're asking, then I guess the answer is yes."

"Just what are you looking for in life, Erin?" His voice was hard and sharp, piercing, cutting, plunging deeper into Erin's sensibilities. "What kind of relationship do you want? Just a few good times, then good-bye. No hard feelings on either side when parting time comes?"

"Put that way, it sounds crude," Erin parried, hurt by his callous accusations.

"I hope so," he grated, "because it's not only crude, it's inhuman. It not only hurts, Erin, but it's humiliating. You ask me to love you. I did! I do! I've given you my best, and I want to continue giving you my best. But what are you giving me? What have you given me?"

Taken aback by his angry outburst, Erin retaliated in a coolly defiant voice. "I never promised you more."

Erin had never expected this from him. She had known that he wouldn't be pleased with her answer, but she hadn't been prepared for violent anger. During the past few months he had been so tender with her, so understanding, so patient. She wasn't prepared for the sudden, total withdrawal.

"Well, did I promise more?" she goaded, replying defensively.

He spun on his heels and faced her, his eyes coolly appraising her. "No," he exhaled slowly, "you never promised me more than a good time in bed, did you?" Erin's mouth flew open in furious amazement, but Devlin didn't stop speaking. His hand shot out, clasping her hand, and he pulled her along behind him as he walked toward their suite. "Then let's not waste such valuable time or such a romantic atmosphere on such mundane topics. The night is young and is made for love."

Erin tried to wrench out of his viselike grip, but he didn't turn her loose, nor did he shorten his angry strides. Easily he made his way across the cobblestone courtyard.

"Devlin," Erin gasped, near tears, trudging behind him, balking, digging her feet into the cobblestones, "don't do this to us. Please, don't!"

"Don't do what?" he lashed out, never missing a step. "Don't be angry because you've used me. Don't be angry because you've thrown my love into my face. Don't be upset because I don't mean any more than a good bedfellow to you." In the lobby now, he slowed his pace, waiting for her to catch up with him, but he didn't turn her loose. Rather he dropped his arm around her shoulder, propelling her up the stairs to their suite. Once there, he shoved her inside and slammed the door. Erin moved across the room, rubbing her hands up and down her upper arms.

Devlin's face was set; it looked as if it had been sculpted from granite. His eyes were cold and hard, unyielding. Gone were the sparks of life and amusement that had swirled in their darkness. Gone were the softness and the tenderness that had warmed them. Determinedly he moved across the room toward her.

She held her hands out, warding him off. "Don't—" she

sputtered, taking a hesitant step backward. "Don't come any nearer."

Devlin laughed, the sound sinister to Erin's ears. "Don't fret your pretty little head, Miss Lindsay. I'm not going to touch you." He stopped walking and dropped his hands to his hips. Contemptuously he surveyed her for a second before he spoke. "But I'll admit, Erin, I would like to touch you. For once I'd like to penetrate that wall of ice behind which you hide. One time that I make love to you, I'd like to know that I'm really touching you." His lips moved into a cruel quirk, a harsh semblance of a smile. "At least when we see each other in the future, Erin, possibly when we think about each other from time to time, if nothing else, we'll remember that we were fantastic in bed."

"My God, Devlin," Erin spat out angrily, finally gaining use of her vocal cords, following him into the bedroom, "you make me sound like a—"

Not letting her finish her statement, he said, "Bitch. And at the moment I think the description fits you." He quickly jerked his clothes from the hangers and threw them in a crumpled heap into his suitcase. He walked to the bathroom.

"What are you doing?" Erin demanded when he returned, dumping his shaving kit into the suitcase.

"I'm packing," he retorted dryly.

"Where are you going?" she cried in a frenzy.

He closed his valise and slung Erin's on the bed, lifting the lid, unceremoniously packing her clothes. "We're going home, Erin. I have better things to do with my weekend than spend them with a selfish woman who won't consider anyone's needs but her own. I'm tired of being frustrated. I'm tired of wondering if you really do care about me or not." Her clothes packed, he slammed the lid shut. "I'm just tired," he sighed wearily.

Erin ran to him, her hand curling over his arm. She

couldn't believe that he would walk out on her like this. "Devlin," she implored him desperately, "let's talk about this."

"Not this time, Erin. We've done too much talking already, and it's getting us nowhere fast."

She moistened her lips. She swallowed, trying to rid her throat of the knot that was growing larger by the second. She wasn't ready for Devlin to leave her completely. She still needed him. She still wanted him. "Give me more time." She sidled closer to him, her voice lowering to a whisper. "Please."

Again he shook his head adamantly, but his expression changed. "Can't." His voice softened, and he reached out, his hand touching her face. "I really can't, Erin. I'm too involved, too committed, and it's unfair to me." Sadly, wistfully, he smiled. "I'm too vulnerable where you're concerned, little angel, and I've got to protect myself. I'm too old for fun and games like this."

"It's not a game," she protested.

- "No?" He dropped his hand. "I wish I could believe you." Without moving he lifted the telephone and dialed. Erin heard him speak. Leaving . . . flight reservations . . . my bill, please. Check out. *No! No! You can't do this to me.*

"This—this isn't good-bye, is it?" Her eyes widened with fear, and her voice shook. "You're not leaving me, are you?"

"No," he answered her softly, a tenderness creeping into his tone, into his eyes. "I'm not leaving you. I'm going to take you back home."

"That's not what I mean," she countered.

His hand reached out and his fingers curled around a strand of hair that wisped around her face. "It's evident that we've never been together, Erin," he explained quietly. "In order to leave someone, you must first have been together, and—" the timbre of his voice changed to a soft whisper "—we . . . haven't."

"What do you mean?" Tears spiked her lashes; they washed her voice.

"I mean that I love you, Erin. I want more than a good time in bed. I'm ready to make a lifetime commitment. In fact, I have made a lifetime commitment, and I want the same from you."

"Why must you insist on this?" she cried out. "Why, Devlin? Why must you ask for more than I can give?"

He hoisted his suitcase in one hand, hers in the other. "Don't worry, sweetheart—" the words were automatic, no feeling emoted "—you're safe. I'm not going to ask for more than you're prepared to give. But neither am I going to accept the crumbs that you're willing to toss me." He walked out of the bedroom, stopping in the doorway. "Let's go."

"Devlin—" her voice dropped to a low, throbbing whisper "—what about our weekend?"

He didn't answer immediately. Instead, he turned and walked into the living room.

"Answer me!" she demanded hotly, her hurt causing her to sound angry. "Damn you, answer me!"

In the middle of the room he stopped, set the luggage on the floor, and reached into his pocket. He pulled out a small envelope and opened it. Holding up an engagement ring, he said, "I don't think you'll like your birthday gift, Erin. And like you said, it's not your birthday. Why pretend?"

He tossed the ring at her. Taken off-guard by his sudden movement, she jumped, and the ring landed at her feet. She bent to pick it up, and tears threatened to pour down her face. Reverently her fingers touched the gold circle; adoringly she looked at the beautiful diamond.

"Oh, Devlin," she sighed, "it's—"

"Keep it," he interrupted. "Keep it for old times' sake.

Now, let's go." Once again he lifted the luggage in both hands, and he moved toward the door, his voice drifting back to where she stood. "You were right, Erin. Remember when we first met. You said that I was the incurable romantic and you were the realist. And I guess it's plain to see that neither of us is going to change." He transferred one of the suitcases from his hand to under his arm. With his free hand he juggled the doorknob, laughing sadly. "I had thought at the beginning that I could empty you of hurt and grief, Erin. I had thought I could love your sorrow and bitterness away. But I was wrong. You enjoy these emotions too much to part with them."

"Devlin," Erin gasped, affronted, "how can you say that!"

Over his shoulder he called. "Instead of creating a heaven of love for us, little angel, I've made myself a bed of hell."

Erin cringed. "Devlin," she cried, grabbing her purse as she raced down the corridor after him, "please, can't you see what you're doing to us?"

He paid no attention to her. "I'm afraid that before my heart is whole again, if ever it will be, I'm going to burn a lot longer."

"Devlin," Erin cried again, running behind him. "Devlin, wait!"

He never stopped. He never answered.

CHAPTER NINE

Devlin unlocked the door and stepped into the house, glad for the coolness of the air-conditioning, glad to escape the heat of the midsummer day. As he walked into the living room, he stopped at the occasional table, setting his briefcase down, and read the note that Mrs. Hooper had left him. Holley had picked the girls up from school and wanted to keep them for the weekend. If it was all right with him, she would bring them home on Sunday. Call either way to let her know. Mrs. Hooper herself was spending the weekend with her son and would see him on Monday morning.

Crumpling the note and throwing it into the wastepaper basket, he flexed his shoulders and moved quickly across the room to the bar. He opened the door of the small refrigerator, extracted several cubes of ice, and dropped them into a glass. After he poured himself a drink, he walked into the bedroom and began to undress.

Another boring dinner engagement, he thought, shrugging out of his navy blazer and hanging it in the closet. He liked the Pruitts, but their dinner parties left much to be desired. It was difficult for him to endure the evening gracefully, mouthing social platitudes. He loosened the knot of his tie and pulled it from around his neck. He could call and cancel out altogether. It wouldn't surprise them. After all, he'd already had to call to let them know that he'd be late.

He walked to the dresser and dropped his tie bar into the jewelry chest. He was unbuttoning his shirt when he heard the doorbell ring. Surprised, he turned his head and looked at the clock. Seven thirty. He wasn't expecting anyone. Again the chimes sounded. He sighed his frustration and quickly strode to the entrance, opening the door, displeasure furrowing his brow.

Shock froze the expression on his face, and he softly sighed, "Erin." He couldn't believe his eyes, and he wasn't sure that he had articulated her name. Dumbfounded, he stood, staring at her.

"Hello," she murmured, her blue eyes openly, hungrily flickering over his face, taking in the surprise that registered in the ebony eyes, the creases in his forehead, the silent glaring.

Devlin's mouth moved again, but he said nothing. He couldn't. This was the first time he'd seen her since they'd returned from Mexico weeks ago. True, they'd been working on the merger of the two companies, but neither of them had met. Deliberately he had refused to meet with her, always sending either Sam or Wally in his place.

Hiding any emotions that would have shadowed his eyes or his face, Devlin studied Erin thoroughly from head to toe. Her hair was impeccably and elegantly coiffed in a smooth roll, and she was dressed in a navy blue pin-striped suit and a white blouse.

"What can I do for you?" The question was formal and businesslike; it was cool and appraising. He evinced no interest whatsoever, and there was no curiosity glimmering in the depth of those eyes.

"I need to talk with you," she replied in a cool voice, wishing he would invite her in.

"I'll be at the office by eight in the morning. Why don't you come by then." His tone clearly dismissed her. "I'm busy at the moment."

"I wouldn't have made this trip over here if I hadn't considered it important," she pointed out.

He crossed his arms over his chest, heaving a sigh of exasperation, and he rocked back and forth on his heels for a while, his eyes traveling over the length of her. "Nothing red," he commented suddenly, taking her by surprise.

Disconcerted, her eyes widened and she stared blankly at him. As many times as she had rehearsed this scene in her mind, she had never written this line into the script. Totally perplexed, she murmured, "What?"

"You're not wearing red today."

She looked down at her suit, shaking her head. "No," she replied faintly, "I'm not."

If she hadn't been so nervous and apprehensive, if she hadn't wanted this meeting to be perfect, and if Devlin hadn't been so austere and unapproachable, she would have told him the truth. She would have grinned and teased him. But she was too unsure of his reaction. And to blurt out that she had on a red half slip would sound too intimate, much too suggestive.

"May I come in?" she asked. When she saw the denial on his face, when she felt his no, she spoke. "As I said, it's very important that I speak with you." She hesitated, but again he didn't answer. "It won't take long, Devlin, and you need to know this before you meet with your directors next week."

"Come to the office Monday," he told her curtly. "Sam and Wally will be there, and they're handling all the details of the merger."

"I don't plan to be in town on Monday," she returned

obstinately. "So it's talk with me now or wait until I return." She stared defiantly at him, her gaze never wavering. "If you don't talk to me now, the negotiations will be delayed indefinitely." She smiled, turning. "It's up to you."

He irritably sucked in a deep breath and released it. Deliberately he crooked his arm and brought his wrist up, looking at his watch. "I can't spare you too much time," he allowed dryly. "I have a dinner date tonight, and—" He left the sentence dangling, letting her fill in the rest, hoping she would think he had a date with a woman.

"It won't take long," she promised him crisply, her heart hurting with jealousy. How callous he was! He was absolutely impervious to her. "Just give me a few minutes." She wondered who his date was. He'd certainly been the focal point of the media recently, and always beside him was a lovely woman. Which one was it tonight?

Seeing that she didn't intend to leave without talking to him, he shrugged and stepped aside, motioning her into the living room. But he didn't follow her immediately. Slowly he closed and locked the door and then moved past her as he walked into the bedroom. "I just fixed me a drink," he explained, his voice receding as he left the room, growing louder as he returned, drink in hand. "May I fix you one?"

"No," Erin replied quickly, shaking her head, glancing around the room.

Devlin inclined his head in acknowledgment. "Do you mind if I dress while we're talking?"

Yes, I do mind! she wanted to shout. *I want your undivided attention.* All she replied, however, was, "No, I don't mind. And—" she added nervously, needing something to soothe the churning in her stomach "—I've changed my mind about that drink. I would like one."

Devlin sighed his exasperation and looked at her for a

full second before he finally nodded and walked to the bar. "What'll you have?"

"A cola, if you have one."

Devlin lifted his brow mockingly, smiled sardonically, but made no caustic remark. Once again he moved behind the bar and busied himself with getting the ice and pouring the soda. He watched her as she ran her hand up and down the edge of the manila envelope that she held. He suppressed a sudden smile that threatened to curve his full lips. Erin was as uncomfortable as he was.

He carried the drink to her. "Here," he said, "you take this, and I'll take the papers."

She smiled and shook her head. "The papers are mine. I just came to talk."

If he were taken aback by her reply, he didn't show it. Rather, he handed her the cola. "Okay. Talk." And he turned, moving toward his bedroom.

Taking a deep breath, Erin said, "When you first approached Joe G. about a merger, he was in favor of it. He didn't think Lindsay Machinery could make it."

Devlin stopped at the doorway and turned, seriously studying her. Something in the tone of her voice alerted him to the magnitude of her discourse.

"And he hasn't changed his mind," she continued smoothly, "but the board of directors has. In the past six months, under my direction, the company has made substantial gain and our creditability has been reestablished. Therefore the board no longer feels the need for a merger."

Devlin shrugged unconcernedly and walked into the bedroom. "Strike three," he called. "I guess I'm finally out of your life completely." So involved with choosing his shirt and finding his socks, he didn't notice Erin standing in the doorway. "But you know, Erin, I still can't understand why you found the merger to be . . ." He never completed his sentence. He looked up and his voice trailed into silence.

He stood transfixed in front of Erin, his shirt parted down the middle, hanging loosely, his stomach and chest bare. His ebony eyes riveted to Erin's face which openly mirrored her hunger and her desire. For endless seconds they stared into each other's faces, then slowly Erin's eyes began to blaze a slow path over him, and even though he still wore his shirt and slacks, she made him feel as if she were touching him physically. He felt shivers of anticipation as they speared through his body, and he felt that deep ache in the center of his being.

Again blue eyes locked with ebony eyes, both staring. Both peered intently into each other's souls, reading an anguish that each shared. Out of the periphery of his vision, Devlin saw the black purse gently thud to the floor, and he saw the manila envelope spill its papers from the other hand. Then he saw nothing but the full beauty of Erin's face.

"Were you against the merger because it was symbolic to your surrendering to me?"

She shook her head. "No, I was against it because I believed in Lindsay Machinery, and I knew that I could make a go of it. I just wanted to be given that chance."

"Looks like you're going to get it," he said softly, taking another step toward her.

She nodded, smiling. "I am." Her heart pounded with apprehension, and she wondered if he were going to give her another chance.

"You drove over here just to tell me this?"

"No," she returned steadily, "I came to tell you that you didn't strike out." She smiled, and although he didn't immediately return her greeting, his firm chin seemed to soften. Then slowly the sensual lips began to move, to lift, and that familiar series of grooves creased around his mouth. "You've just hit a home run," she told him, "and bases were loaded. And it's the top of the ninth inning."

Standing in front of her, he reached out, his fingertips tracing the gentle rise of her cheeks. "Do you know what's going to happen, Erin?"

"Yes," she whispered, fearing that he would take her body but would want nothing more. She feared that he wouldn't want all of her, which is what she could now offer him.

His fingers touched that soft, vulnerable indentation at the base of her throat. "Dear, sweet Erin, I still want you." The pain of his confession stung him, but it didn't diminish the ache of desire that surged through his body.

His words, washed with anguish, hurt Erin so badly that she closed her eyes. "And I want you," she mumbled thickly.

"I know," he soughed sadly, dropping his hand, simply standing and looking at her.

"Most of all, Devlin," she continued, slipping the button of her jacket through the loop, sliding the thin wool off her shoulders, unmindful that the jacket fell to her feet. "I love you." Never taking her eyes from Devlin's face, she unbuttoned her blouse, letting it, too, flutter to her feet to land on top of her jacket. Her fingers deftly, adroitly, unzipped her skirt, and it joined the heap of discarded clothing. "This is what I came for today. I wanted to say I love you."

He heard the words, but he didn't acknowledge them. He moved, catching her close to him, so that she felt every muscular inch of his body. The tangy warmth of his breath caressed her as he bent his head toward her with that old familiar slowness that was both infuriating and exciting. His lips, full and soft, at the same time rough and hard, came close, then moved away, brushing her lips, tantalizing them until she ached for the moist heat of his mouth. Again his lips brushed hers.

"I've waited a long time for those words," he murmured. "I'm glad now that you insisted on coming in."

"Love me, Devlin," she whispered, closing her mind to his omission, surrendering to the desire that swept like liquid fire through her veins. A band of sorrow and fear tightened around her heart, constricting her breath, but, at the same time, she experienced that same sweet expectation that she'd known so many times before with Devlin. A thousand memories swept through her mind; a thousand feelings that she had tried to repress and to forget inundated her. "Please, love me," she pleaded fervently.

"Hasn't it always been that way," he murmured, moving her so that she was leaning against the doorframe, his lean body trapping hers, pushing against it.

Erin welcomed with pleasure the weight of his lean body against hers. It was so much more delightful than she had remembered. That wild, fierce joy surged through her, bringing her to life, igniting her affections, letting her love burst into one great flame for Devlin to see, to feel, to share.

"It's been that way," she admitted faintly, her hands slipping under each side of his shirt, pushing it off his shoulders, "but is it that way now?" As she waited for his answer, she ran her hands over his sinewy back, up and down the gentle contour of his spine.

"Yes, darling," he told her, smiling gently, "it's still that way." His lips trailed across her cheeks to her lips. "I don't know why I was so mule-headed, sweetheart. I've done nothing but punish myself for these past weeks." He pulled back and laughed into her face. "And I'm old enough to know better than that."

"What about your dinner engagement tonight?" she asked, the thought coming from that far island of remembrance. But she didn't care if he answered or not. That it may be another woman didn't bother her. She was here with him now, and she would make him forget. She would make him love her again.

"What about my dinner engagement?" he parried, easing away from her, looking at the creamy expanse of skin above the lacy fluff of her bra. With a gentleness that was reverent and adoring, he bent his head and kissed her above first one breast, then the other. A sudden erotic chill shook her to the core of her being. Her body, remembering the sensual contour of those questing lips, wanted more than kisses. Her body, remembering the ecstasy of complete fulfillment, demanded total possession.

Her rising desire vibrated through her body, taking residence in her throat, coming out as a soft sound of need. When Devlin heard the sough, he raised his head and a slow smile touched his lips and his face. Again he eased himself away from her, his hands sliding down her arms, his hand clasping her hand. They walked to the bed together. She saw the love shining in his eyes; she saw the tenderness and the gentleness of his face.

She would tell him now. "Devlin, I—"

Afraid of what she was going to say, and not wanting to hear it, he placed a finger over her mouth, quieting her. "You don't have to say anything, sweetheart," he whispered softly. "This time we'll just take what few moments of happiness we can find when we can find them." Even though it hurt him to say the words, he had finally accepted that Erin would never make a commitment. "I don't understand your values, darling, but perhaps you're right. At least they must be right for you. Perhaps I've been selfish in demanding too much from you."

She shook her head and would have told him differently when he lifted his fingers from her mouth, but just as she started to speak, he capped his hand over her mouth again. "No more words, angel."

Then he dropped his hand and began to undress while Erin stood staring at him, unable to utter a word. How she wanted to speak. She wanted to tell him that during the past few weeks she had learned that she did want a total involvement with him and the girls. She wanted love, and she wanted a family. She wanted to make and to keep promises. She wanted to give him her absolute devotion and fidelity. And she had learned that she wanted the same from him. A one-sided love was miserable.

When she opened her mouth a third time to confess these thoughts, Devlin shook his head. "I said no more words," he reminded her, his mouth closing over hers, strangely more tender than she had remembered. He drove the remainder of her hurt and anguish away, replacing it with his tender touch. Forgetting her confession, she met his kiss with her own mouth, soft and eager, pouting for his touch.

"No more words, my darling," she sighed when he lifted his mouth and drew away from her. "Just loving from now on." She lifted her hands, cupping his head, holding his lips to hers, and she sent her tongue into his mouth, probing and exploring the warm, moist depth.

A shudder of passion racked his body, and his hands first tightened, then loosened their grip on her shoulder. With smooth motions that never interrupted their sexual interplay, Devlin eased her onto the bed. "Just loving," he repeated gently, slipping her underwear off, holding her slip in his fingers for a few minutes. "Ahh," he discovered, "you did have red on after all."

As the fabric fluttered to the floor, Erin said, "I did."

His fingers drifted to the rise of her breasts, and he brushed the feminine peaks enticingly before he lowered his face, his mouth gently circling first one then the other. Erin arched, thrusting them more fully into his mouth, aching for his touch, for his love, for the piercing warmth of his masculinity.

His tongue teased the sensitive tip with a delicate and tentative touch, and a sharp shiver of pleasure riveted through her. Her hunger for him welled from deep within; her needs and wants surfaced. She gasped, and she clung to him, promising herself that she would never let him go. She would convince him of her love somehow. She would. She invited him at first, then she begged him to continue his ministrations. She didn't have an ounce of pride left. Now she understood Devlin's vulnerability.

When his mouth withdrew, his fingers began another assault, and his lips followed the new campaign, touching her closed eyes, softly kissing the lids. He drew away, and his fingers stilled their movement. Erin, bereft, opened her eyes, which were fevered and glazed from her wanting, and she looked into the face that hovered above her. She saw the desire that glowed in his eyes, and she looked deeper. She searched for love, but she couldn't find it. She had no way of knowing that he had deliberately hidden it. But, no matter, she would accept whatever he offered.

Softly she smiled, and he smiled. Then, almost as if he had made a decision, his mouth began to forge a path from her throat downward to the smooth roundness of her breast that had grown tighter and fuller to the touch of his hand. She tilted her head back in a silent plea for his caresses, for his butterfly kisses. He answered her prayer. He kissed her until she was dizzy with wanting; then he turned his face, letting his cheek rest against her breasts. His hair touched her naked, sensitive skin, sending another shaft of want through her body.

His mouth continued to torment her as he made his way downward. His lips brushed against the softness of her stomach, and Erin's lower body ached and throbbed with her need. Arching her back, tangling her hands in the thickness of his black hair, she moaned her desires to him. Freely she offered all of herself to the questing touch of his mouth.

"Devlin," she breathed heavily and raggedly. "Now, please. Don't make me wait."

He moved, his hands anchoring him above her, his knee separating her legs. Gently he lowered the weight of his body on her, one hand moving to her thighs, preparing her for his entry. Her hands cupped his face, and she brought his lips to hers, opening her mouth for the thrusting invasion of his tongue as his body settled on hers, his masculinity burrowing into her silky warmth.

She moaned deep in her throat, and she lifted one of his hands, pressing it to her aching, swollen breast. Their coming together was volatile and desperate, and it excluded tenderness. Neither could exercise control; neither wanted to draw their pleasure out. Urgency drove them both on, and passion swept them beyond their depth. All restraints were cast aside.

Then their desire, reaching the highest pinnacle possible, exploded, and they burst into small particles, sailing into space, gliding, floating up, then down, then up, a peacefulness finally descending on both of them. Fears and doubts were swept away. No words were spoken, but their bodies communicated totally. Love spoke, and both of them understood. Both knew. Later, much later, after they had eaten, they would talk.

Clad in Devlin's robe, a glass of wine in her hand, Erin perched precariously on a barstool. She swallowed the last bite of her sandwich and crunched on a few more potato chips. When she looked up, Devlin was leaning on the counter, propping his weight on his elbows, his eyes gleaming with amused patience.

"And what are you grinning at?" she demanded pertly.

"You," he said, his eyes sweeping down to her breasts. He reached out to pull the robe together. "You're coming out."

She smiled and looked at him, her eyes gazing lovingly at the full length of his lean, muscular frame. Clad only in his pajama bottoms, nothing was left for Erin's imagination. Her hand reached out, and her fingertips feathered across his stomach just above the elastic of his pajamas, then below the elastic.

She whispered, "You're coming out too."

"What are we going to do about this?" he asked.

"Do you have any plans for the weekend?" she asked, slipping off the barstool, looping her arms around his neck.

"Nope."

"What about the girls and Mrs. Hooper?"

"The girls are staying at Holley's, and Mrs. Hooper is going to stay with her son and new grandson for the weekend."

Her smile broadened, and her fingers locked together at the base of his head. "I think perhaps for starters we ought to spend the weekend together."

He chuckled. "My sentiments exactly. Your place or mine?" Before she could answer, he said, "Probably your place. If you stay here with me, we'll have to go get your clothes."

Erin shook her head, and her eyes sparkled with mischief. "Nope! We won't have to do that." He cocked a brow quizzically. "My bag is already packed."

"That sure of yourself?" he teased.

She shook her head. "No, actually I was quite unsure of myself, but I hoped." The blue in her eyes deepened. "And I believed you. I believed you when you said that you'd made a lifetime commitment."

His arms tightened around her, and he drew her nearer to him, burying his face in the sweet curve of her neck and shoulder, inhaling deeply of that fragrance which was Erin. "Do you want me to go get your bag out of the car tonight, or shall I wait until morning?"

She eased herself back, pulling her shoulders away from him, but keeping the lower part of her body against him.

"There's something else that I'd rather we did this week-end."

"What?" he asked curiously, searching her face for some clue to her request.

"I'd like for us to return to Mexico."

Devlin tensed and his eyes narrowed. It was too soon, and he wasn't sure what kind of relationship they were beginning. "I—don't think—"

Erin put her fingers across his mouth and hushed him. "I've already booked us a flight, and I've reserved our suite." Again he shook his head. "This time I've booked us the same suite that we had there before." Still he didn't look too pleased with her suggestion. "Next time," she said, her voice dropping to a faint whisper, "we'll book the bridal suite." Now she waited on tenterhooks for his reply.

"Are you sure?" he asked, his eyes enigmatic and blank, no emotion glowing in them.

"I'm sure," she returned softly. "I love you, and I want to be your wife." He smiled, and for the first time that evening she saw the warmth of his love which outshone his desire and passion but didn't obliterate either one. "Will you marry me?"

"No more doubts and fears?"

"Maybe," she confessed truthfully, "but our love is so great that I'll overcome them. Furthermore," she added, "I can't live without you. It's almost as if you've branded me, Devlin." Her eyes misted with tears of happiness. "Now, give me an answer. Will you marry me?"

"Yes, my darling," he murmured, "I'll marry you."

Of one accord they turned, walked out of the kitchen, switched off the light, and moved to the bedroom, lost in the paradise of their love.

Candlelight
Ecstasy Romances™

$1.95 each

At your local bookstore or use this handy coupon for ordering:

DELL BOOKS
P.O. BOX 1000. PINE BROOK. N.J. 07058-1000   B182A

Please send me the books I have checked above I am enclosing $_____ (please add 75c per copy to cover postage and handling) Send check or money order —no cash or C.O.D.'s Please allow up to 8 weeks for shipment

Name _____

Address _____

City _____ State Zip _____